Praise for Jackie Ashenden

"Ms. Ashenden's storytelling talents continue to keep me on the edge of my seat, only wanting more when the book ends. If you are in the mood for a well-written erotic romance, read this book."
—Harlequin Junkie Book Reviews on *Having Her*

"*Living In Sin* is a twisted and complex story of breaking down walls, of facing the hard truth, and accepting that life isn't always easy but when happiness is offered it is okay to reach out and take it."
—Guilty Pleasure Book Reviews

"With characters you care about and some scenes that will make you sweat, this title is definitely sexy."
—Library Journal Reviews on *Taking Him*

Look for these titles by Jackie Ashenden

Living in Secret

Jackie Ashenden

SAMHAIN
PUBLISHING

Samhain Publishing, Ltd.
11821 Mason Montgomery Road, 4B
Cincinnati, OH 45249
www.samhainpublishing.com

Living in Secret
Copyright © 2015 by Jackie Ashenden
Print ISBN: 978-1-61922-798-9
Digital ISBN: 978-1-61922-222-9

Editing by Christa Soule
Cover by Lyn Taylor

First Samhain Publishing, Ltd. electronic publication: February 2015
First Samhain Publishing, Ltd. print publication: June 2015

Dedication

This one's for Christa, my amazing editor. For pushing me to do better with every book. You rock.

Chapter One

Connor Blake stepped out onto the tiny balcony that led off from the conference room and closed the double doors behind him. The sound of the Auckland Law Society's Friday night after work drinks was cut off and replaced by the hum of city traffic.

He paced over to the rail and leaned his elbows on it, gazing down at the street below and all the people hurrying home from work or wandering in groups, looking for places to eat or drink.

God, he needed a cigarette.

For some reason he was finding the usual drinks and networking thing difficult tonight and he had no idea why, especially when he was normally more than happy to grease the social and professional wheels for a couple of hours.

Are you sure you don't know why?

Connor slowly clasped his hands together, shifting his weight.

Maybe he knew. Maybe it had something to do with the papers still sitting on his desk at work. The divorce papers Victoria had sent him. They'd been sitting there a month and he still hadn't signed them. And that he *really* didn't understand.

He and Victoria had been separated a year. There was no reason for him not to sign those papers. No reason at all. Yet still he hadn't.

Christ, why the hell had he given up smoking? Stupid idea. Especially now, when he could really murder a cigarette. But cigarettes were one of the vices he'd given up back before he'd started law school, along with a number of other…temptations. He didn't do those things now, not anymore. In fact, there were many things he didn't do anymore. His law firm—he, in particular—took on a lot of police prosecutions, and that involved setting a certain example. In fact, he was renowned for his spotless reputation, a reputation he cultivated as assiduously as a rose grower did prized flowers.

However, avoiding temptation did nothing for the urge. The urge didn't change. He only managed it. And only if he was very lucky, would the urge go away.

So far, he hadn't been lucky.

He turned from the sight of the city streets, back to the double doors leading into the conference room, currently full of lawyers talking shop or comparing golf handicaps and the dreadful state of Auckland's house prices.

And froze.

Through the glass of the doors, he saw a group of people move and shift like a school of fish, revealing a familiar figure. A woman in beautifully tailored black pants and jacket, a deep red blouse in dramatic counterpoint glowing against her olive skin. Her coal black hair was pulled back in a tight bun on the back of her head, glossy and smooth as a slick of oil.

Victoria. His soon-to-be-ex-wife.

Turn away.

A gut punch of something hot and raw hit him, but he locked it down instantly, the way he'd been doing for so long he barely even registered it anymore. In fact it was odd that he was aware of it now, because even though he hadn't seen her in the flesh for six months, he was perfectly fine with that. They'd both agreed it was better they stay away from each other, give each other some space and time to move on. And as far as he was concerned, that's exactly what he was doing. What was done, was done, and he was moving forward with his life. Just as she was.

Victoria was talking to Craig Matthew, a senior partner in one of Auckland's biggest company law firms. Connor had only just finished speaking with the man himself, having to put up with some unwanted and unneeded advice about the prosecution he was currently dealing with—an eighteen-year-old charged with the murder of his father. Matthews had informed Connor that he'd been following the case with interest and had decided Connor and his team weren't hungry enough and that Connor wasn't asking the hard questions.

A patently ridiculous conclusion. There was no one hungrier for justice than Connor and his team. And as for the hard questions, well, that was because he hadn't even started asking yet.

He realized his hands were in fists. He unclenched them.

What the hell was Victoria doing here? She never came to the drinks, not these days.

Turn away. Turn the hell away.

But he couldn't seem to bring himself to do so.

She was smiling at Craig, her generous mouth full and red. She'd always been exquisitely beautiful and she still was. Except there was a certain spiky edge to her usual regal poise that hadn't been there before, and she looked…tight. Tense. Like she was constantly bracing herself for a blow that never fell.

Except it did fall. You remember that.

Oh yes, he remembered. Coming home one day to find a letter sitting on the kitchen table. A letter from a girl who was apparently the daughter Victoria had given up for adoption when she was sixteen. A daughter he didn't know she'd had.

She'd claimed there had been cracks running through their marriage for years, that her daughter's sudden appearance was only the final hammer blow to break them apart.

But if there had been cracks he hadn't been aware of them. He'd thought they were solid. And it wasn't Jessica's advent that had shattered them, but the fact Victoria had kept secrets from him. And rather than talk about it, she'd walked away.

She'd been the one to go. She'd been the one to ask for a separation. And now, finally, she was the one who'd sent the divorce papers.

The hot feeling in his gut twisted. Anger.

He found himself reaching into his jacket for a packet of cigarettes that hadn't been there for nearly twenty years.

Jesus. What was wrong with him? He wasn't angry with her, not now. Yes, he'd been furious when she refused to talk to him, when she'd wanted some time apart. But he'd agreed to the separation. Agreed to the distance she'd wanted. And it was behind him now. He was looking ahead as he always did.

Turn away, you fool.

She tilted her head as she talked, her strong, determined chin lifting. The expression on her face was all polite friendliness and professional interest. Contained and restrained. Doing her networking thing because she'd always been ambitious. The usual Victoria, in other words.

As she had been when she'd thrown that half-assed bullshit at him about him wanting her to be perfect all the time and how she could never live up to his impossible standards. Which was crazy. He'd never wanted perfect. He'd just wanted her because she was perfect already.

"Until you found out I had a child. Now I'm not so perfect anymore, right?"

"It's not about the child, Victoria. It's about the fact that you didn't tell

me."

"*Oh so we're going to have that discussion, are we? How about you tell me your secrets then, Connor? We can start with why you have a sword tattooed down the middle of your back.*"

Impasse. Because it was true he had his secrets, but they were the kind he told no one. The kind he protected people from. And they were going to stay that way. But an unexpected child was different. And most especially when she'd told Connor she didn't want kids.

Connor folded his arms and leaned back against the railings, consciously letting the tension in his shoulders and arms seep away. No, he wasn't going to turn away. He'd look. He'd watch her because he felt nothing for her anymore.

Nothing at all.

Then Victoria turned and like she'd known he was there all along, her gaze met his through the glass.

Dark eyes. Liquid black. Endless, fathomless.

And that gut punch struck again, precise as a bullet, smashing through all the carefully constructed walls and barriers he'd built around himself and his appetites. Walls and barriers created to keep temptation at bay.

Connor didn't move. Didn't look away.

He was wrong. It wasn't done. Because it was still there. That deep, intense hunger. That visceral pull. The one he'd fought and locked down since the moment he'd met her, keeping it in the box where he put all his baser, more primitive emotions. A survival skill he'd learned over twenty years and practiced until it became instinct.

He didn't know why it hit him so hard in this instant, why he was so aware of it now. But one thing he was sure of: he didn't want it.

Turn away.

No, it was too late.

She was coming toward him.

Victoria knew Connor was there. Even as she talked with Craig, asking meaningless questions about the case he was working on. Questions she barely took in the answers to. Mainly because every ounce of her awareness was concentrated on the door that led out to the tiny balcony. And the man behind it.

It had taken her at least ten minutes of walking around and chatting to people to realize he wasn't in the room. Then as she'd got waylaid by Craig, she'd felt a familiar prickling sensation. A pressure. A steady, creeping heat making its way over her skin.

Connor.

She always felt that way when he looked at her, when his blue-laser stare focused unerringly on her. As if she was the only person on the entire planet. She used to think he only looked at her that way, that she was the lucky one. But he looked at a lot of things that way, as it turned out. Things he found interesting. Or annoying. Or puzzling. Not that it was easy to figure out which one of those things it was since Connor was the world's most difficult man to read.

Whatever, his stare always made her heart beat faster, made her mouth go dry, though she made sure she didn't let that show. Because God, it made her angry. That even after what had happened between them, she still wanted him.

But then she'd felt that way for a while now and that's why all of this was so hard.

She bore the stare a few moments before bracing herself and turning to look in his direction.

And as usual she felt the impact of those intense eyes as a blow, echoing through her like the aftershocks of an earthquake.

It never used to be like this. He'd always been a beautiful man but it was his reserve and his detachment that had been the main attraction for her. She didn't want passion or chemistry, thunderbolts or lightning. A meeting of minds was infinitely preferable to a helpless meeting of bodies because she knew where that led and it was nowhere good.

Connor had been safe. She admired his mind and his ambition, and that's all she'd wanted.

And then things had changed. And he wasn't quite so safe anymore.

Victoria swallowed, a shiver going right through her.

He looked the same as he always did, his dark blue suit beautifully tailored and his red and blue silk tie perfectly straight. His white shirt was spotless, his black hair styled conservatively. The sharp, aristocratic lines of his face gave him a hawkish look, predatory in some lights, especially when he was in the courtroom.

That had been when it all started, this hunger.

She'd come into the public gallery on a whim, wanting to see her husband in action during a particularly tough domestic violence case.

He'd been there, laying out his argument, and that's when she'd seen it, his famous reserve and self-containment drop for a moment. When he'd paced back and forth in front of the jury, lean and dangerous as a hunting cat. Fixing each of the jurors with that focused stare as he spoke, his deep voice losing its usual cool, becoming hot, seductive.

As she watched, the jury became mesmerized by him.

And so did she.

Now, with the intensity of his gaze on her, she had that same sense of being mesmerized. Like a snake in front of a snake charmer. There was something in his eyes that was different though. Something…

No, God, she had to get it together. Remember what she came for. And if she kept looking at him any longer, she was going to give something away and there was no way in hell she was going to do that.

With a supreme effort of will, she looked away from Connor and began finishing up her conversation with Craig. It didn't take long. Then, allowing herself at least a minute to make sure her emotional armor was firmly in place, she began to head toward the balcony where Connor was standing.

He wasn't looking now and had turned around, his back to the glass doors. A tall, dark, broad-shouldered figure, his hands braced on the iron railings of the balcony.

She let herself have a second to study him unobserved, because it had been six months after all and as much as she didn't want to acknowledge it, the sight of him made her feel breathless. Made her heart beat fast. A dangerous indulgence…

Victoria blinked. Took a steadying breath. Then pushed open the doors and stepped out onto the balcony, closing them behind her.

Connor didn't turn. "So," he said, his voice cool and dark, and very calm. "I wondered what you were here for. I suppose it must be important if you're willing to risk a face-to-face meeting."

She realized she was holding her briefcase in front of her like a shield. Damn. Forcing herself to drop it to her side, she replied in the same calm tone, "It is important. I sent you a couple of emails but—"

"I've been busy." Again his tone was cool.

"You didn't reply to my voicemails either."

Slowly, Connor turned around. He didn't say anything, his cornflower gaze sweeping over her, impersonal and arrogant. As if he was a king and she was a supplicant begging for favors.

By rights it should have made her furious and in a way it did. But not because she didn't want him to look at her like that. It was because she did. Because it made her ache, made her breathless. And *that's* what made her angry. God, she hated it.

Only years of practice at hiding her emotions let her meet his gaze without even a flicker. She merely raised an eyebrow. "I suppose you've been too busy to listen to those too?"

He leaned back, long fingers curled around the black iron railings. "This is about the divorce papers, isn't it?"

There was no point dancing around the subject. "It's been a month, Connor."

"Like I said. I'm in the middle of an important case. I've been busy."

"And I need them signed. Since I couldn't get through to you any other way, I thought a personal visit might speed things along."

"I didn't realize there was a deadline."

She hadn't told him of her plans. After all, why would she? They weren't any of his business. Still, it was only polite he be aware of the fact she was planning on leaving the country.

"And I didn't realize it was going to take you a month to sign them." She gripped the handle of her briefcase tighter. "I've had a job offer from a firm in London and I'd very much like to take it. In fact, I'm hoping to leave in a few weeks or so. Which means I'd like to have a few loose ends tied up before I go."

The look on his patrician features was impenetrable. "Loose ends such as an eighteen-year-old daughter and a divorce?" There was no emphasis in his voice, no discernable emotion. It was offered in the same, calm tone as he always used. The same as when she'd asked him for a separation and he'd replied "if it's what you want".

"Yes." She kept her expression as neutral as his. "Such as those."

"I see." Another cold sweep of that impassive stare.

A tense, familiar silence fell. One she remembered from those days before Jessica had sent her letter. Full of all the things Victoria couldn't say, couldn't give away. He never gave any sign he found these silences as difficult as she did, but then it was obvious he hadn't experienced the same sexual epiphany about her that she'd had about him.

They hadn't shared a bed for three months before the separation and he hadn't seemed to find this difficult in any way. And that hurt. Even though she'd been the one to pull away from him. She just hadn't been able to stand the cold, almost perfunctory couplings that had been their sex life, not now she wanted him. It was a bizarre position to be in, to want one's husband and yet not being able to stand his touch. Because he didn't touch her like a woman he wanted, more as if she was a duty he had to perform.

Well, he wasn't going to have to perform that duty any longer.

Victoria lifted her chin. "The papers, Connor. I need them signed before I leave."

And she wasn't sure what it was, but she saw something flicker in his eyes. Something that wasn't cold or impassive or detached. A spark. He stared at her, the spark slowly gathering heat. "And what if I don't want to sign them?"

Her stomach clenched and for a second she didn't quite know what to say since that was *not* the response she'd been expecting in any way, shape or form. "What do you mean, 'what if I don't want to sign them'? I thought we'd agreed that if we're still separated after a year, we'd make it permanent."

"I'm aware of what we'd agreed."

She didn't understand the look in his eye or the strange, hard expression on his face. "Are you telling me you've changed your mind?"

"I haven't said anything of the kind. I only asked a question. Which you haven't answered."

"You have to sign them, Connor."

"I don't *have* to do anything, Victoria."

She stared at him, frustration coiling inside her, along with a fair degree of puzzlement. He'd let her go so easily when she'd suggested they spend time apart, after he'd confronted her with Jessica's letter. It had been the only time she'd seen him anything less than composed and to be honest, it had surprised her. Because over the past couple of years of their marriage, she'd got the impression that she wasn't so much as wife to him as an accessory to his career. To be fair, he'd always given that impression and initially, that's exactly what she wanted since he was her accessory too.

They'd been like colleagues, workmates. Their discussions mostly revolving around their jobs: the prosecutions the police contracted to his firm and the growing field of technology law that was her specialty.

Separate bedrooms and mostly separate lives.

But ever since desire had screwed everything up, she found she wanted more than that. And part of her had been hurt he hadn't wanted to fight for her. Then again, why she had expected anything different, she couldn't understand.

Connor's perfect reputation was important to him and he'd wanted the perfect wife to go along with it. A woman with a past and a child she'd given up for adoption when she was sixteen was not perfect.

"So…you won't sign them?" She studied his face, looking for clues. And that too felt familiar. Seemed like she was always watching him, looking for a hint, anything that would give her some insight into what he was thinking or feeling.

"I'll sign them when I'm ready and not before."

Frustration gave way to anger, but she swallowed it down the way she always did. "Let me get this straight. You're quite happy to have a separation but now you don't want to sign the divorce papers because…?"

He lifted a shoulder as if unconcerned, yet the spark in his gaze was slowly gathering more and more heat. "This case is taking up a lot of my time, and quite frankly I have a lot of other things to do that take precedence."

"All they need is a signature, for God's sake."

"Which I'm not ready to give just yet."

Her mouth tightened. "That's extremely inconvenient."

"I'm not here for your convenience."

"No and you never have been." She couldn't stop an acid bite from tingeing the words. "Only for your own."

The spark leapt in his gaze, a bright, intense flash of blue. Anger.

A shock of surprise went through her. Why the hell was he angry? Surely he wanted this divorce as much as she did?

"You're right," he said coldly. "This is for my own convenience. And it's not convenient for me to sign those papers yet."

"Then when?" A little devil twisted inside her. "I would have thought you'd be chafing at the bit to get rid of me." She allowed herself a smile. "After all, you were quite happy to let me go."

Connor didn't move. "You were the one who decided to leave, Victoria."

"And I got no arguments from you."

"Because I respected your choice."

Because you didn't care.

The words echoed in her head and she had to look away in case his sharp gaze could read them in her eyes.

"This is an old argument," she said, staring past him, over the city and the skyscrapers glittering in the last of the early evening sunlight. "And it's pointless to have it again. Just sign the papers, please. I want them back to me in three weeks." She began to turn.

"I'm not signing them," Connor said, and this time, beneath the smooth, cold darkness of his voice, Victoria caught a hint of something else. A slight roughness that hadn't been there before. "Not yet."

She stilled and turned back.

And the silence that fell between them now felt different. Charged in a way she hadn't experienced before, at least not with him.

Heat crept over her skin, a prickling sensation like an electric field passing over her. Because he was looking at her the way he'd looked at those jurors in the courtroom. With intent, determination. Like a hunter spotting prey.

The breath caught in her throat and she could feel the heat begin to intensify, a burning wave sweeping over her, making her want to run and hide, and yet get down on her knees in front of him at the same time. And along with the heat came the shock.

She'd always thought he was a passionless man and it had only been in the past couple of years she'd gotten hints he wasn't quite as passionless as he'd made out, only very, very locked down. She'd just never expected to see that passion directed at her.

Which made it doubly important that he sign those papers and for her to get out and away from him. He was no longer the safe option and the quicker she got away from him the better.

"Whatever it is you're holding onto," she said, keeping her voice cold, "you'd better let it go. It's over, Connor."

His eyes gaze held hers, and for a second that hot, blue spark was all she could see. "No, Victoria," he said softly. "It isn't."

Chapter Two

Connor sat at a table near the bar in the Ivy Room of the Auckland Club, the exclusive private members club that his friend Kahu owned. It was Thursday night, which meant drinks with Kahu and Eleanor, his other law school friend, plus their respective partners.

He normally enjoyed Thursday nights. It was a chance to catch up with his friends and relax, let the leash slip a little. He'd been especially looking forward to it this week since the murder case he was working on was tough and had been occupying rather more space in his brain than it should have.

Yet he found he just couldn't relax like he normally would have. He was wound up, antsy and tense.

It was all Victoria's fault. If she hadn't turned up at the Law Society drinks the week before, if she hadn't turned her back on him and walked out, he would have been fine. He certainly wouldn't have had this inexplicable anger burning dully away inside him like the embers of a smoldering fire. An anger that had prompted him to say things he'd never meant to say. Like telling her he wasn't going to sign those papers. Like telling her it wasn't over.

Stupid bloody thing to say. Because it *was* over. And no wonder she'd turned her back on him and walked out without another word. She knew a lie when she heard it. So why the hell had he said it in the first place?

"You're particularly broody tonight," Kahu said, taking a sip of his beer and eying him. "Or maybe pissed is more accurate."

"I'm not pissed." *Damn liar.*

His friend's dark, skeptical gaze gave him the once over. "Still haven't signed those divorce papers, huh?"

Connor had told Kahu about Victoria's divorce proceedings in a moment of weakness. He didn't normally share things like that with his friend, mostly because once you'd started with one secret, pretty soon you'd spill all of them and there was no way he was going down that road. Certainly he regretted telling Kahu, mainly because he didn't want to have to explain why he still hadn't signed the papers. Jesus, he couldn't even explain that to himself, let alone someone else.

No wonder last week Victoria had looked at him like he'd just dropped in from Mars. And that had made him even angrier. He wasn't used to explaining or justifying himself, and the fact that he felt so oddly inarticulate in front of her had been fuel to the fire inside him.

Being inarticulate was not a good trait in a lawyer.

It hadn't helped he'd also been so very conscious of her perfume on the balcony, a complex, subtle scent beneath the fumes from the road below and the salt on the air from the sea. Over the years he'd made himself ignore it so that these days he barely even registered it. But something to do with his anger and her turning up out of the blue like that had triggered a sudden, intense awareness of the smell of magnolia blooms and rain, like a tropical thunderstorm, full of sharp static and drowned flowers.

He didn't want to be conscious of that scent. Or of the way that deep red blouse of hers had pulled across her breasts when she breathed in. Or the way her mouth, almost the same color as her blouse, had tightened when he'd told her he wasn't signing her papers.

His desire for her was a need he'd conquered years ago, so he shouldn't have been so physically aware of her now.

And yes, that failure had made him angrier still.

So he'd said no. Told her he wouldn't be signing her damn papers. And he didn't give a damn whether she was leaving the country or not, he'd sign those papers only when he was good and ready. And he wasn't ready.

You want to punish her.

The thought made him extremely uncomfortable so he ignored it.

"No," he said flatly. "I haven't signed the papers."

Kahu took another sip from his bottle. "Why not?"

His friend's gaze had shifted to the woman behind the bar, a small, slender strawberry blonde who was currently standing on the tips of her Converse sneakers as she chatted with Eleanor, also at the bar ordering more drinks. Lily, Kahu's young dancer.

Connor hadn't approved and he still didn't, not that Kahu gave a damn about his approval. But there was something about the open hunger in his friend's eyes whenever he looked at Lily that Connor found appalling.

You're not appalled. You're jealous.

"Because I haven't," he said tersely. "Do I need a reason?"

"I suppose not." Kahu's attention flickered back to him once more. "Maybe the real question isn't whether you've signed the papers. Maybe the real question is why are you so angry?"

Connor opened his mouth to reply.

"And don't tell me you're not angry, you fucking liar," Kahu said before he could speak. "I know you, man. You hide it well, but I know when you're angry."

Connor shut his mouth and took a sip of his own beer instead. "Where's Luc?" he asked, changing the subject. Eleanor's partner had just passed his bar exams and apparently there was going to be some kind of celebration. Connor didn't approve of Eleanor's choice either. Luc was much younger and far more intense than was good for any person. Plus he had an air of tightly leashed violence around him that made Connor instantly wary.

Then again, the man was fiercely protective of Eleanor for which Connor gave him a pass. And as for Lily, well, apart from her age which he thought made Kahu seem faintly ridiculous, he had nothing against her. Except that since she'd gotten a position in a ballet company in Sydney, it meant Kahu would be selling the club and moving there to be with her. Which was all very nice for Lily, but Connor couldn't see what Kahu was getting out of the deal.

"He's having an interview with some firm or other," Kahu said carelessly. "And don't change the subject." He paused, his gaze turning uncomfortable. "What did she do?"

Connor didn't need to ask him who he meant. For a second he sat there, then realized he was fiddling with the beer bottle in his hands. Uncharacteristic for him since he wasn't normally a fiddler.

Damn, did he really have to have this conversation? Ah hell, might as well say something. Kahu wasn't going to be around for too much longer after all and the guy already knew about the divorce proceedings.

You tell them one thing, pretty soon all the rest comes out too...

Connor ignored the thought. "She turned up at the Law Society drinks last week."

"Uh huh. Don't tell me. She wanted to know why you hadn't signed the papers too."

"Yes."

"And you said...?"

"I'd sign them when I was ready."

Kahu's mouth turned up. He seemed to be all about smiles these days. "Jesus Christ, Connor. Anyone would think you don't actually want to divorce your wife."

The bottle in his hands was starting to get warm, half the label peeled away. He put it down on the table. "She's the one who wanted the divorce, not me."

"So you don't want to divorce her then?"

The anger simmering inside him began to come to a slow boil. He put his hands on his thighs, trying to relax his fingers. If he ignored the emotion, eventually it would go away. That's what happened with most emotions. "What I would like is to move on."

"Fucking hell. Sign the papers then."

Connor let out a slow breath. Then he met his friend's gaze. "I still want her, Kahu."

The other man frowned. "I don't see the problem. Fuck her. Then sign the papers."

"Jesus, as if it's that easy."

"Sure it's that easy."

Connor glanced over at Lily, who was now turning in a slow pirouette at the bar, Eleanor grinning at her. "It may have been that easy for you, but it's not that simple with us."

Kahu's grin changed, as if he was thinking of some kind of private joke. "Easy is a relative term, I guess. Okay, maybe I see your point. But I still don't get the problem."

"It's not like we're friends anymore. We're separated." Connor didn't want to explain the fact that physical passion had never played a part in their marriage, especially to Kahu who before he'd fallen for Lily, had been one of Auckland's biggest playboys. Kahu's usual modus operandi had nothing to do with restraint, while his own... Well, restraint was his whole life. It was better that way.

Except for now. Except for her.

She'd always been the exception. Which was why he'd married her.

Because if he could beat his hunger for her, he could beat anything. And he had beaten it. For five years he'd ignored it and pretty soon he'd ceased to feel it anymore.

Which made it strange he kept thinking about it now. Perhaps it was the fact he hadn't been with a woman since he and Victoria had split up. There had been plenty of opportunity, but first he'd been too busy at work and then… Then he just hadn't been interested.

"Okay, again, so what?" Kahu picked up his bottle again, waved it at Connor. "You don't have to be friends for a good screw. You only have to both feel the same way. So…does she?"

Good question. Did she? She'd never given him a sign that she did, not once.

Do you even want to know?

Another good question. Because if she did feel it and knew he did too…

Once again a hot, raw sensation burst through him, the deep pull of desire that had his breath catching. Christ, this shouldn't be happening.

"No," he said curtly, ignoring that too. "I'm pretty sure she doesn't."

"That's a shame." Kahu sipped meditatively at his beer. "Because you know, if she did, you might want to organize yourself a nice little arrangement."

Connor narrowed his eyes. "What kind of arrangement?"

The other man smiled. "The kind of arrangement where you fuck away your feelings."

"Jesus."

"What? I hear it works."

"And naturally you're speaking from experience."

Again the other man's gaze went to the woman behind the bar, the look in his eyes softening. "Yeah. But it didn't work out for me so well. I got stuck with my feelings."

Clearly this was a good outcome judging by the expression on his friend's face. But it wouldn't be for Connor. He didn't want to be stuck with the anger. Or the desire, for that matter. What he wanted was for both to be gone so he could get on with his damn life.

Then again…

What have you got to lose?

"Got a buyer for this place yet?" he asked, another graceless change of subject.

Kahu didn't take his eyes off Lily. "An old friend of mine is keen. He's just getting the finances together and then he's going to make me an offer."

Connor paused. "Are you sure you want to sell?"

His friend flashed him a grin. "I'm sure. Like you, I want to move on. But this time it's going to be moving on to something different. Something new."

"In Sydney? Really?"

Kahu laughed. "It's not Sydney that makes it different, mate. It's Lily." He finished his beer, put it down on the table and gave Connor a brief, meaningful look. "And I don't think you quite understand that yet, do you?"

Connor stared at him. "What are you talking about?"

Kahu shook his head. "With any luck, you'll find out. Now, if you'll excuse me, I need to go help Lily with her…stretches." He got up from the table and Connor watched as he strode through the tables and crowds scattered around the room, heading toward the bar.

And he kept watching as Kahu rounded the bar and came up behind his slender dancer, putting his hands on her hips and pulling her close. She smiled, lifting an arm to wind up and around his neck. Eleanor said something, making Lily laugh. And Kahu's arms slid completely around her, holding her as if she was something precious.

Connor tore his gaze away, a strange feeling in the pit of his stomach. Like loss or grief, he couldn't tell which.

Either was a problem and either he didn't want.

At that point, his phone buzzed in his pocket. He reached down and pulled it out, glancing down at the screen. A text from Victoria of all people.

Will you be going to the last fling party?

A second passed where he wondered what on earth she was asking him then he remembered. Kahu was throwing a party here at the club. He hadn't wanted a goodbye party, settling for a "last fling" party instead, which Connor had to admit, was far more appropriate for Kahu.

It was promising to be a big one, for members only, prompting a flurry of membership applications Kahu had duly turned down. He'd hinted to Connor it was likely to be the kind of party Connor would find "uncomfortable". Which meant something sexual no doubt.

He'd still planned on going because Kahu was a friend and he'd been going to the Auckland Club pretty much since Kahu had taken ownership of it.

Yes, he texted back.

Okay. I'll let Kahu know I won't be there then.

Connor stared down at the screen and her reply, feeling that anger turn over inside him once more. *He'll be disappointed if you don't come,* he texted back.

You'll be there. We agreed on distance.

He cursed under his breath, texting back a quick response. *It's one night, Victoria. I'm sure we can manage one night.*

And he meant it. Kahu would be disappointed if either of them didn't make it and hell, surely they could both handle a couple of hours for one of their closest friends?

There was a long pause and he wondered if perhaps she wasn't going to reply. Then at last his phone chimed a response.

Okay. One night. We don't have to talk to each other.

No, damn straight they didn't.

His phone chimed again.

I'm still waiting, Connor.

He bared his teeth at the screen and typed out a quick response.

See you at the party, Victoria.

Then he turned his phone off.

"What about this one?"

Victoria looked up from the rack she was sorting through.

Eleanor had her hand outstretched, holding up a dress that looked more like a scrap of red silk than it did an actual dress. It was an off-the-shoulder number, very short, and was the deep red, nearly black of the darkest, most expensive of red rose petals.

Victoria wouldn't wear it in a million years.

"Seriously, Ell?"

"Oh come on, it's perfect."

"You wear it then."

"I've already got mine sorted out." Eleanor cast another glance over it. "You can't deny it's sexy."

Victoria turned back to the rack of clothes she was examining. "I don't do sexy. You know that. I'm not even sure if I'm going to go anyway."

She and Eleanor had spent most of the day looking for a dress for Victoria to wear to Kahu's party, a futile mission as Victoria had kept pointing out to her friend since she probably wouldn't go anyway. But Eleanor had been adamant. She was "fucking going to Kahu's party", and she was "going to wear a sexy fucking dress".

Victoria didn't particularly want to do either but it looked like she wasn't going to have a choice in the matter, at least not about attending the party. Kahu was a very old friend. She couldn't not go to what was ostensibly his farewell party.

Pity Connor was also going to be there.

She set her jaw, ignoring the sudden burst of anger flowering inside her at the thought of him. He was being a grade A bastard about signing those papers and she *still* didn't know why.

It's not over...

Why on earth would he think that? When he'd made no effort to talk to her or see her, or even discuss their separation with her for over a year. It was as over as a marriage could be so why he thought any different, she didn't understand. Not when he'd never given her even one sign that he wanted them to stay together.

She jerked a hanger along the rail, looking sightlessly at the next dress on the rack. It was black. Plain. A high neckline and longer sleeves. Mid-calf length. Very conservative and pretty much exactly what she was looking for.

"Oh fuck no," Eleanor said from behind her. "You're not trying that thing on. I forbid it."

Victoria let out a slow, silent breath. "It's more me."

"Yes, it is. Elegant. Classy. Conservative. And there's nothing wrong with that, believe me."

She turned and met her friend's direct gray eyes. "I can hear the 'there's everything wrong with that' in your voice, though."

Eleanor's gaze was uncomfortably sharp. "Okay, I'll be honest here. I'm worried about you, Vic. You're working a lot and you've lost weight. And..." She stopped. "I don't want you to go to London."

Victoria had told her friend a month or so ago about her plans and Eleanor had been unimpressed. In her usual direct way, she'd told her that leaving was not going to solve her problems. Which presupposed there were problems to solve and there weren't.

Only a long lost daughter who had turned up out of the blue and a husband who refused to sign the divorce papers.

Jessica was not an issue—the letter Victoria had been sent had been short and to the point. A brief note to explain she was well, she was with a family who loved her and she loved them. That she wanted to reassure her mother she was okay. She hadn't left any contact details, which indicated she didn't want Victoria to return the contact and Victoria was okay with that. Her daughter was safe and well, and that was all that mattered.

And as to the husband…

"I know you don't want me to go. But the job is a good one and—"

"It's not about the job. This is about Connor, isn't it?"

Victoria turned away, uncomfortable. She slid the black dress along the rail, looking at the next one along. She didn't want to have this discussion. Didn't want to tell her friend the truth about her marriage. Eleanor had had her own difficulties with her ex-husband, Piers. And though Eleanor had never given her the details, Victoria knew they were pretty serious ones. So she'd never shared her own about Connor, because suddenly falling in lust with your husband three years after you'd married him seemed a ridiculous thing to complain about.

It would also mean exposing her initial reasons for the marriage and that too seemed like a step too far. She would have to fess up about Jessica and she wasn't ready to tell the world about her daughter yet. Not when it had gone so spectacularly wrong after Connor had found out.

"He won't sign the papers," Victoria said eventually. "And he's had them a month now. I went to see him personally about them last week and he refused point blank. He wouldn't even give me a reason."

"So? Make him then."

Victoria turned around. "I can't make him, Ell."

Her friend was staring at her, blonde brows drawn together in a frown. "Of course you can. There must be something he wants that only you can give him. All you have to do is tell him he can't have it unless he signs those papers."

There were many things Connor Blake might want. Unfortunately, despite being his wife of five years, she had no idea what they could be. Oh, there were the obvious things, like his passion for becoming a crown prosecutor. For making his firm, Blake and Associates, the leading private law firm in Auckland. Becoming a QC. All career-oriented things. But that was the extent of her knowledge of his desires and dreams. They'd never shared any others.

At her silence, Eleanor's frown deepened. "You can think of something he wants, right?"

"Yes," Victoria answered reflexively.

"All right. And you should probably wear this dress when you talk to him because it'll look damn hot on you." Eleanor wrinkled her nose. "Actually, on second thought, maybe you'd better not wear it. He might never sign those papers if he sees what he's giving up."

A kernel of guilt settled in her stomach. "It's not his fault," she said. "I'm the one who gave up the marriage."

She'd always been careful to make sure people knew that. Not giving them the whole truth about Jessica being the catalyst and certainly not revealing her real reasons for walking away from Connor, but citing the fact that they'd changed and both wanted different things. He'd never refuted her and for that she was glad. It was easier not to go into detail for either of them after all.

"Yeah, but he didn't exactly go after you, did he?" Eleanor pointed out.

"He respected my choice. That's what I wanted."

But her friend's gaze was shrewd and far too perceptive. "Are you sure that's what you wanted? I mean, yeah, choice is important. Actually, it's vital. But sometimes, in certain situations, it's nice to have it taken away from you too."

There was a look in Eleanor's eyes Victoria found both fascinating and yet somehow threatening at the same time. Like her friend knew something she didn't. "What do you mean?"

Eleanor only gave her an enigmatic smile and thrust out the red dress. "At least try it on."

It wasn't her kind of dress. It showed too much skin and that split promised bad things. But what the hell. She supposed trying it on wouldn't hurt, and at least it would get Eleanor off her back.

With a sigh, she took it into the fitting room and got rid of her suit. Then she pulled the dress up and stared at herself in the mirror.

The dress was actually quite beautiful, the fabric petal-soft and light against her skin. But it clung to her hips and thighs in a way that was almost indecent, plus she was right about the split. It went all the way up to one hip meaning her underwear would be on show. The way it gathered on one shoulder would also require a strapless bra, which was annoying.

She shifted uncomfortably.

"I'm disappointed, Victoria. This is not what we brought you up to be. We expected better of you than this…"

She blinked at the echoes of her father's voice in her head. Why on earth was she thinking of him now? Especially those sad, disappointed words he'd thrown at her the morning he'd caught her sneaking back into the house after she'd been out all night. At the time his sad disappointment had hurt worse than anger because she'd always hated letting her parents down. Especially when they worked so hard to give her better opportunities and had so many plans for her.

She'd only disobeyed them once, creeping out of her window to go to the school dance. They hadn't wanted her to go or wear the short sexy dress she'd chosen because that's what the other girls were going to be wearing. But she'd been sick of their rules and limitations. Sick of being suffocated by the need to be equal to their impossible standards. She'd only wanted a little fun.

But there had been consequences to that fun. Consequences that had nearly ruined her life.

Victoria met the gaze of the woman in the mirror. A tall woman, too thin. Wrapped in deep red silk. With a dark, fathomless gaze. Enigmatic, full of secrets.

A stranger in a sexy dress that emphasized the curves she still had, breasts, hips and thighs. Sexual. Sensual…

A shiver went through her.

She'd always put herself under pressure to do things well. To be successful. To not make any mistakes. And all because of Jessica and what she'd had to give up.

Because she had to make that sacrifice mean something.

And if it was a chance at having the kind of successful life her parents had planned for her then that's what she had to do. Otherwise she may as well have disobeyed them and kept her baby.

You should have done that anyway.

Ah, but there was no point in thinking that. She hadn't kept her. Her parents had told her Jessica would have a better life with people who could afford to look after her properly. Who could give her all the opportunities and advantages Victoria wouldn't be able to. And they were right. She wouldn't have been able to give her daughter what she needed, which made giving her up for adoption the right thing to do.

Victoria reached up behind herself to undo the zipper on the dress.

"Are you ready?" Eleanor asked from outside the fitting room curtain.

"No." She began to tug down the zipper. The dress could go back on the rack. It *really* wasn't her.

There was a pause and suddenly the curtain was jerked back, Eleanor standing in the doorway, one hand on her hip. "Hmmm. I knew you were lying."

She could feel a flush creeping into her cheeks as her friend gave her the once over, unexpectedly and uncharacteristically self-conscious. "I can't wear this. It's not me."

"You keep saying that. And, yeah, maybe not."

Victoria blinked. "Well, I'm glad you—"

"Connor will *never* sign the papers if you're wearing that dress. He'll also never want to let you out of his sight."

A jolt went through her, like an electric shock. The thought of Connor's eyes on her, following the line of her figure, the spark she'd noticed at the Law Society drinks getting hotter and hotter…

She turned sharply back to the mirror, breathless.

You want to be a bad girl…just once more…

Only to meet her friend's perceptive, gray gaze reflected back.

"Ah," Eleanor said softly. "So it's like that, is it? You *do* want him to see you like this."

Victoria put her hands on her hips, smoothing down the fabric, using the motion as an excuse to look away. "I couldn't care less if he saw me or not." But even to herself the statement sounded false.

"Hey, Vic. It's me," Eleanor murmured. "What's going on between you two?"

"There's nothing going on."

"I'm your friend. Don't lie to me."

She didn't want to explain, but it had kind of gotten past the point of no return. Damn her friend for knowing her so well.

Giving the dress one last smooth, she said, "All right. Don't get me wrong, I do want the divorce and I'm going to go through with it, but…" Finally she raised her head and turned, facing Eleanor directly. "I still…

want him, Ell."

There was a brief silence.

"Well, that's annoying," Eleanor said. "Seeing as how you're separated and everything."

The understatement made Victoria smile reluctantly. "You could say that."

Slowly, the other woman came into the fitting room and made a spinning motion with her hand. "Turn around."

Victoria did so then felt Eleanor pulling at the zipper on the dress, tugging it back up again, closing the fabric back around her.

"So," her friend said after a brief pause. "Why not have him?"

Oh, there were many reasons why not. Most of which she wasn't going to talk about in a fitting room in a dress shop because they were too complicated. But there was one she could give Eleanor, a reason that didn't need any complex explaining. "Because he doesn't want me."

In the mirror she could see a skeptical look cross Eleanor's face. "Are you sure?"

The spark in his eyes as he'd looked at her. The thick, dense energy between them.

But that couldn't be what she thought it was, could it? He'd never wanted her, not really and not in that way. Because if he had, surely he would have stopped her when she walked out the door?

"It's not over, Victoria."

"Yes," she said. "No. I don't know."

Eleanor stepped back. "I think you should find out for certain."

"Why? What's the point? I'm not changing my mind about the divorce."

"I wasn't suggesting that." Her friend's smile was only just a tad short of evil. "I think you should find out because then you might have something you can use to make him sign those divorce papers."

For a second, Victoria wasn't quite sure what she meant. Then she realized. "You mean sex?"

Eleanor look amused. "Of course I mean sex. What else did you think I meant?"

She could feel her mouth start to get tight. God, she really didn't want to talk about this either. Sex had always been a difficult subject ever since she'd been sixteen, after that night at the school dance where she'd been seduced by Simon Curtis in one of the dark halls near the girl's bathrooms. She'd given in so easily, amazed by the power of the feeling that had gripped her, the intensity of the need, the ferocity of the pleasure. It had been like a whole new world opening up to her. So much so she hadn't even realized he hadn't stopped to put on a condom until after it was all over.

It had shocked her that she, a good girl who knew all about safe sex, could be so blinded by the needs of her own body. And perhaps if there hadn't been consequences, she wouldn't have worried so much. But there had been consequences, devastating ones, and ever since then she simply hadn't trusted herself enough when it came to men.

She'd tended to stick with men with whom she had little chemistry, sex perfunctory and at least not actively unpleasant, keeping herself in control at all times.

Which had made Connor so damn perfect. Until she'd seen him in the courtroom…

"You're looking prudish again," Eleanor observed. "You should have been a Puritan, Vic. It would have suited you."

She looked away, back to the mirror where that woman stood, a siren in a slinky red dress. Definitely not a Puritan. "I'm not sure that's a good idea," she said. "What if he says no?"

Eleanor shrugged. "Then he says no and you have to think of something else. But…honestly. I don't think he's going to say no."

That's not what you're worried about. You're worried about him saying yes.

Another hot jolt went through her and in the mirror she saw a dusky blush rise to her cheeks. Because what if he did say yes? What if he did want her after all? And not just in that somewhat mechanical, detached way he had when they were in bed. But in a way that was hotter, more intense. Demanding. The way he was when he was in the courtroom, when he was trying to seduce the jury...

"I'm not sure it would be worth it, though," she said, half to herself, conscious that her voice wasn't exactly level. "The sex has never been great."

"Well, isn't that up to you?" Her friend sounded very matter of fact. "You don't have to accept things the way they were. You can change them." This time her smile was downright wicked. "And if not, then you can just get drunk and screw someone else. Which also works."

"You know, you're sounding more and more like Kahu every day."

"Since he's buggering off across the ditch to Sydney, someone's got to." Eleanor raised her eyebrows. "Are you going to buy the dress or not?"

Victoria swung round. "I'm going to buy the dress."

She might not wear it when the time came, but at least she'd have options.

When it came to getting what she wanted from Connor, she had a feeling she'd need every single option she could find.

Chapter Three

Victoria sat in her car and watched her ex-husband get out of the taxi. He was in a black suit tonight and a shirt the same electric blue as his eyes. He had on a black tie that was, as usual, perfectly centered and knotted. He always dressed well, did Connor.

As she watched, he bent to the driver's window to the give the driver some money, before straightening to his full height. Tall. So very tall. Taller than she was. Long and lean, built like a gymnast. He kept himself in shape by running and lifting weights in the gym he'd had installed in their home.

Did he still do that? He must because it looked like there wasn't an ounce of fat on him.

A hot feeling shifted inside her.

As he went up the steps and disappeared inside the club, she let out a shaky breath and looked away, smoothing her hands over the silky fabric covering her thighs. The dress felt suddenly far too tight, her skin far too sensitive.

Perhaps she should have worn a different dress instead. Then again, it was too late now. She'd spent at least thirty minutes standing in front of her closet door, debating the merits of whether to wear the red dress or not. Finally, she'd decided to put it on, but not for the reasons Eleanor had suggested.

Her friend thought Connor wouldn't be able to resist her wearing a dress like that.

But Victoria knew her husband better than that and the sad fact was he'd probably be *more* likely to let her go if she wore that dress.

He preferred restraint. Classy sophistication. Definitely not the kind of blatant sexuality this dress showcased.

The reality was if he saw her in this, he'd probably be shocked. Appalled even.

Which was perfect. Shocked and appalled was far more likely to sign the papers than restrained sophistication.

She looked down at the red silk pulling tight around her thighs and the hip-high split revealing the black lace of her panties. Really, it was the kind of dress you had to not wear anything underneath if you didn't want to spoil the line of it.

God, what would he think if he knew she was wearing no underwear? He'd probably be even more shocked and appalled.

Victoria swallowed. Then, not letting herself think too much about the decision, she reached up and wiggled her panties down her legs. It was moderately awkward—her Audi was spacious but didn't allow much room for panty removal—yet seconds later, she had her panties in the glove box and nothing but bare skin between herself and the silk of her dress.

Her insides felt shaky, her heartbeat thumping in her head.

She pulled open the door and got out, smoothing down her dress again and locking the car. The early summer breeze stirred against her legs, reminding her of what she didn't have on underneath, and she had to pause, leaning against the cool metal of the car.

What the hell are you doing? Everyone's going to see you in that dress and they're going to know you have nothing on underneath it.

But that was good, wasn't it? More incentive for Connor to sign those papers and get rid of her. And as for other people and what they might think, well, she'd be gone in a few weeks anyway. She'd start again in a new city where no one knew her.

A clean slate.

Victoria eased herself away from the car and turned.

The Auckland Club, the building wreathed in ivy, its famous blue door shut, looked quiet and still. A staid reminder of times past. But it wasn't either of those things. She could hear music thumping, the sound of laughter. A party in full swing. She'd never been to the more outrageous parties Kahu threw from time to time, finding the blatant sexuality of them uncomfortable. Connor hadn't liked them much either and for the same reason.

And yet, that look in his eyes...

No, it wasn't what she thought it was. She'd been imagining things. Connor had never wanted her, not in that way, and he never would. The only thing he had a passion for was the law. Justice. And that was it.

She braced herself then walked forward up the steps to knock on the door. It swung open almost immediately to reveal Mike, the Auckland Club's bouncer. His eyes widened as he looked at her and much to her horror, she felt herself blush.

"Wow," Mike said. "Hot dress, Victoria."

She managed a cool smile as he ushered her in. "Thanks. Is Eleanor here yet?"

"Yeah. She's in the Ivy Room." He paused. "Though I'm not sure you should go in there."

"Why not?"

He grinned. "You'll probably get mobbed."

Again, she could feel herself blushing. Ridiculous. "I'd better be careful then," she replied, thankful some other people arriving behind her took his attention away.

Perhaps the dress idea was stupid. Perhaps she should never have worn it.

The vaulted foyer of the club, with its massive chandelier, was full of people so she threaded her way through the crowds to a small hallway that led down the back to the bathrooms and Kahu's private study and offices.

There was a small alcove near the bathrooms, with a loveseat positioned to provide a quiet space for those who needed a break, and mercifully there was no one already sitting there. So she sat down, taking a few deep breaths and trying to get a handle on the nervousness and doubt roiling inside her.

If this was going to work, she had to push herself. Be determined about it, no half measures. And that should be easy given she'd been determinedly pushing herself for years now. Yes, it was true, pushing herself to be successful at her career was a different prospect to pushing herself to shock her ex-husband. Using her sexuality in this way was new to her. But that didn't matter. What mattered was getting those papers signed. So she could be free.

"Are you okay?" The voice was deep and soft, and very masculine, penetrating the noise of the party easily.

Victoria looked up.

A man stood in front of her. He was impeccably dressed in a black suit and white shirt, no tie. The shirt was open at the neck, revealing a patch of dark olive skin, and his black hair was long enough curl over the collar. He wasn't typically handsome, but there was something about his rugged features that made him compelling nonetheless. Perhaps it was his eyes, green and gold, like a cat's.

He smiled, his teeth very white in against his tanned skin. "You're

Victoria Blake, aren't you?"

She frowned. "Do I know you?"

"No, we've never been introduced." He held out a hand. "Allow me to do the honors. I'm Raphael Scott, a friend of Kahu's."

Victoria took his hand, slightly startled by the sudden warmth flooding through her as his fingers closed around hers. She tried to ignore it, giving him the same cool smile as she'd given Mike. "Nice to meet you."

His smile deepened. He held on to her hand only slightly longer than was perhaps polite before releasing her. "And you. Kahu's told me a lot about you and your other friends."

Her fingers tingled. She put them in her lap, clasping her hands together. "Oh? He's never spoken about you before."

"No, possibly not. I've been in the States for the past few years, only came back home last week." He looked at the space next to her and raised a brow. "Mind if I sit down?"

Perhaps the strange tingling in her fingers should have made her wary, but for some reason it didn't. There was something completely non-threatening about him, something to do with the warmth in his eyes and in his smile that put her at ease. "Sure," she said. "Be my guest."

Raphael sat down beside her and leaned forward, his elbows on his knees, his long blunt fingers interlaced. "You should probably know I'm going to buy the club. I made Kahu an offer before I came back here and if he knows what's good for him, he'll take it."

Ah, she'd heard about the offer. Eleanor had told her. "Oh, well, that's great. I actually don't come here a lot, but I'm glad it's going to a friend of his."

"Can I ask why you don't come here a lot?" His smile was self-deprecating. "I don't mean to pry, but from a business perspective…"

"Of course. I'm just not much of a nightclub person."

"And yet you're here tonight."

"Well, yes. Kahu's a friend and this is his last party."

"Forgive me," he said, "but for a person who isn't into nightclubs, you're certainly dressed like one."

Again she felt the embarrassment rise, the sting of heat in her cheeks. She looked down at her hands. "Ah, yes, that…"

She could feel him looking at her, but he didn't say anything. A small silence fell and for some reason, it wasn't at all uncomfortable.

Then he said, "Come on, let's go get a drink. You look like you could use one."

Victoria lifted her gaze from her hands and met his green-gold eyes. Heat lurked there, definite heat. A genuine appreciation that intensified her blush.

And an idea took hold. What would Connor think of her walking into the Ivy Room in a poured-on dress and no panties, on the arm of this man? What would he think if she sat down and had a drink with Raphael? What if she flirted openly with him? Would that shock Connor? Appall him? Enough so he'd sign those papers without any kind of argument at all?

It's not just about the papers. You want a reaction…

She shut the thought down. The reaction she wanted was his disapproval. That's all.

So she looked into Raphael's eyes and smiled back. "Sure. That would be great."

"Holy fuck," Kahu said.

Connor turned his head, puzzled by the surprise in his friend's voice. They were sitting in a corner of the Ivy Room, the quiet, classy restaurant it was during the day now turned into a loud, crowded, chaotic club. All the tables and chairs had been cleared away, replaced by long couches and cushions and low tables. Candles in colored glass tea-light holders flickered, glinting off Middle Eastern lanterns hung from the ceiling. Down one end of the room, a slightly raised platform had been constructed as a dance floor. It was crowded now as people danced to some fast, frenetic bass music.

There was an atmosphere of decadence in the room, of opulence and excess. Sensuality and sin. Kahu's favorite combination in other words.

It wasn't Connor's scene in the slightest, but he was bearing it for his friend's sake and because, eventually, Victoria would arrive.

"What?" Connor asked, looking in the direction of Kahu's surprised stare.

The door of the Ivy Room had opened to admit some newcomers, Kahu's friend Raphael, who'd been introduced to Connor when he'd first arrived, and beside Raphael a tall, slim woman in the tightest, sexiest red dress Connor had ever seen.

"It's Victoria," Kahu said, his voice barely audible above the music. "At least...I think it's Victoria."

No, it wasn't. She'd be in her usual evening outfit—an elegant black dress, a bit of gold jewelry maybe, black pumps and her hair in a smooth chignon. Classy, sophisticated and understated.

She definitely wouldn't be in a dark red off-the-shoulder number that looked like it had been poured on. Nor would she have worn her hair like that, a riot of thick, glossy black curls cascading down her back. The shoes, high red silk platform sandals, with straps around the ankles, were far too obvious for Victoria as well. In fact, the whole outfit was far too obvious for Victoria. Which meant it wasn't her, but some poor woman out looking for an easy hookup.

Connor opened his mouth to tell Kahu it definitely wasn't Victoria when Raphael leaned in to talk to her. She turned her head toward him to listen, and Connor felt everything slow down and stop. Frozen.

Because it *was* Victoria. There was no missing that determined jawline and delicate chin. The long, straight line of her nose and finely drawn eyebrows. The full, lush shape of her mouth, carefully colored with lipstick as deep a red as her dress.

Shock coursed through him.

Jesus. What the hell was she wearing? What the *hell* was she doing coming here looking like that?

She and Raphael turned toward the bar, moving over to it. There were a couple of free barstools and he pulled out one for her. She got onto it with her usual elegance, and as she did so, the fabric of her dress parted in a side-split that went all the way to her hip.

Connor felt like he'd been punched in the face. Because there was nothing marring the smooth olive skin of her thigh and hip. No telltale strip of lace. Which meant she wasn't wearing panties.

"Wow, I've never seen her in anything like that before," Kahu observed. "She looks fantastic."

No, she didn't. She looked like a damn prostitute.

Look away...

But he couldn't. She was leaning over to talk to Raphael now, the mass of her thick, curly black hair falling over her shoulder as she put a hand on the guy's knee to balance herself. And he wanted to go over there and rip her hand away. Ask her what the hell she was thinking? Coming in here, wearing *that.*

Anger morphed into fury. Because he could feel his hunger for her shaking the bars of the cage he'd put it in, desperate for release. It didn't want to ask her questions. It wanted her down on the floor beneath him, that dress ripped and her legs wrapped around his waist, those heels digging into his back.

Christ.

Raphael had put a hand over hers and, as Connor watched, he must have said something amusing because Victoria laughed. And even through the noise in the room, the conversation and music, he heard it. A full, rich, uninhibited sound.

The fury twisted inside him. He'd never heard her laugh like that before. She'd never laughed like that for him.

Aren't you not supposed to care?

"Are you okay, mate?"

It took him a second to realize Kahu was speaking to him. That he'd been staring at Victoria and Raphael without a word for at least a couple of minutes.

He tore his gaze away from the couple at the bar. "Of course I'm okay," he snapped. "Why wouldn't I be?" Victoria was obviously trying to prove some point in that getup but whatever it was, he didn't care. He really didn't give a shit.

Kahu said nothing for a moment, his gaze uncomfortably perceptive. "Uh huh. Hey, I've got a new bottle of vintage Laphroaig you might want to try. Come and have a dram with me?"

He didn't want to have a glass of whisky with Kahu. He wanted to talk to Victoria. Tell her about his plan for the "arrangement" Kahu had mentioned last week and see what she said. But he'd been expecting to do that in a quiet, private place with the Victoria he knew, not the courtesan at the bar who currently had her hands all over the knees of another man.

His jaw tightened. He hated it when he had to change his plan of attack due to unexpected circumstances, but what could he do? As much as he wanted to, he couldn't go over and speak to her now, not with this fury beating in his blood. Because he wasn't at all sure he could keep a lid on it. He didn't even fully understand quite why he was so furious in the first place.

He was going to have to go with Kahu. He was going to have to retreat. But maybe it would be for the best. After all, the night wasn't over yet, not by a long shot.

"Okay, fine," he replied shortly. "Lead the way."

Kahu gave a short nod then got up, threading through the crowds and heading toward the doors. Connor followed him, keeping his attention firmly on the exit. But just before he left the room, he couldn't resist once last glance toward the bar again.

She was looking at him.

And once again he felt it, the gut-punch to the stomach as her dark eyes met his. The heat in his veins igniting like a match to a line of gunpowder.

Victoria smiled. It was only a slight, subtle curve to her lovely mouth, but he saw it all the same. And knew it for what it was. A challenge.

Deliberately he turned away.

Very well. Game on.

"He doesn't look very happy." Raphael observed.

Victoria swallowed. Her heart was thumping hard in her chest, a strange electricity sparking in her blood. "No, he wasn't." Her voice was husky as she turned back to the bar, her hands almost shaking as she clasped them in her lap.

Perhaps she shouldn't have smiled at him like that, but she just hadn't been able to help herself. Connor had been furious, no doubt about it, a spark of pure rage lighting in his eyes. And she didn't know exactly what had been the source of his anger, whether it was the dress she was wearing or the way she'd been acting with Raphael, but that almost didn't matter. What counted was getting a reaction out of him that wasn't polite interest or cool friendliness and that was a victory all by itself.

You didn't come here to get a reaction. You came here to get him to sign those papers.

True. But making him angry was a start, wasn't it? After all, if she got him angry enough, perhaps he wouldn't even argue.

She reached out to pick up the glass of wine Raphael had ordered and took a healthy sip. It was cool and dry, delicious.

"You want to make him angry, don't you?"

She didn't look at him for a moment, taking another sip of wine to cover her surprise at the question. Then carefully she set the glass down again and looked at him. There was no judgment in his cat-green eyes, only curiosity. "He's my ex-husband," she said, hoping she didn't need to explain further.

"I know who he is," Raphael replied. "Kahu introduced me to him earlier."

"Well then."

One corner of his mouth turned up. "I get the impression things are not as over as they appear?"

"Oh?" She positioned the glass on its coaster. "What makes you say that?"

"The look he gave you. And the fact he was extremely pissed with me." Raphael paused. "Though I get the feeling you were giving him plenty of ammunition."

Guilt shifted inside her. "Yes, well, I apologize for that. It's a… private argument. I didn't mean to drag you into it."

"I didn't mind. You can put your hand on my knee anytime." There was an unmistakable heat in his eyes that even she, with her limited experience, was able to interpret.

Attraction.

Disturbed and yet at the same time oddly thrilled, Victoria looked away, picking up her drink again and taking another sip. A long time since a man had shown any interest in her and normally it would make her run a mile. Especially when she felt the pull of attraction herself.

But she was starting to think perhaps things would be different tonight. In another couple of weeks she'd be going to London, flying away from her past and all the mistakes she'd made. So what did it matter what she did tonight? As long as she got her papers signed, as long as she was free, that was the only thing that counted, wasn't it?

She put down her glass, looked at her hands spread flat on the bar top. On her left ring finger was a pale, fading line, the mark from where her wedding ring used to be. The line was almost gone. In another couple of months, she wouldn't be able to see it at all.

"Will you help me, Raphael?" she heard herself ask. "I'd very much like to make my ex-husband even angrier than he already is."

There was a brief pause. "And you want to use me, I take it?"

"Yes." She steeled herself. Turned to meet his eyes. "Would you mind?"

He looked at her a long moment and she had the impression he could read her as clearly as words written on a page. It should have felt exposing, but for some reason it wasn't. "Can you tell me why?"

Victoria let out a breath. She didn't want to tell him, but it didn't seem right not to do so, especially when she'd asked for his help. "I want him angry enough to sign the divorce papers."

"I see. And you think making him jealous will help?"

"Well, having you here with me certainly didn't make him any less angry."

"True." He smiled, and there was warmth in it plus a touch of sweetness that calmed her uncertainty somewhat. "But I'll tell you right now the look he was giving me was definitely a 'hands off my property' look. And that's not a look you generally get from ex-husbands."

She should have been bristling at the thought, because she wasn't Connor Bloody Blake's property and never had been. Yet a deep part of her found the statement thrilling in a way she wasn't prepared to contemplate quite yet.

Ignoring it, Victoria arched a brow. "Oh, I don't think so. Connor isn't possessive."

Raphael's smile deepened, like he knew something she didn't. "Sure he isn't."

"He isn't," she insisted. "So, are you going to help me or not?"

"Of course I'll help you." Raphael picked up his own glass and knocked it gently against hers. "I'm a fixer. And I especially like it when I can fix things for beautiful women."

"And you don't mind if I...." She couldn't quite bring herself to say it.

"Put your hand on my leg? Flirt with me? I think I can bear it." Something gleamed in his eyes. "And if I reciprocate?"

An illicit shiver crept through her. She ignored that too. "Well, that would be appreciated."

"Ah, that I can do, darling. That I can do very well indeed."

Connor sat in the deep armchair, his eyes half closed. Christ, he'd had a hell of an evening. His head was spinning from all the whisky Kahu had plied him with, whisky that hadn't done a thing for the anger still burning away in his gut.

Kahu had given Connor a number of conversational openings while they'd sat in his study, his concern for him obvious. But Connor had taken none of them. He didn't want to talk about it. Not about his anger, not about his desire, not about Victoria, period.

Eventually Kahu had taken his not-so-subtle hint and the two of them had rejoined the party in one of the upstairs bars.

It was quieter up here, less noise, fewer people. The room was all red walls and black wood on the floor, with chairs covered in rich, black velvet. There was a small bar along one wall, with a couple of people sitting on black velvet-covered barstools. Other groups of people were scattered on couches or in armchairs. There was even a full-on chaise lounge with a TV star and her entourage sitting around on it.

The music was of the quiet, classical kind, setting the atmosphere for conversation and privacy rather than the noise and chaos of downstairs.

Connor found it much more restful. At least he had. Until the door had opened and Victoria and Raphael had come in.

In fact, if he opened his eyes a bit more, he could see them sitting in a pair of armchairs in the corner of the room opposite him. She'd put her hand on the arm of Raphael's chair and was leaning in to talk, her hair trailing over his knees.

It pissed him off.

He'd been trying to get himself into a calmer state before he approached Victoria but that calm seemed to escape his grasp whenever he saw them. And he really couldn't understand why.

He'd never been possessive. Victoria had never been his property, she was a smart woman with her own choices to make and he didn't own her. In fact, he prided himself on the fact he'd never felt possessive or jealous. And since they'd split up, well, he didn't expect her to remain faithful to him in the slightest.

So he couldn't think of a single reason for feeling so damn angry every time she put her hand on Raphael's thigh or leaned in close to speak to him. So damn furious when Raphael laid a hand over hers or put his mouth near her ear to talk. It shouldn't matter to Connor at all. And yet somehow, it did.

Connor wanted to tell Kahu to call his asshole friend off, but that would give away far too much and he wasn't prepared for that. It was one thing to admit he was angry to himself, to realize he was jealous, quite another to admit it to another person. Especially when he wasn't supposed to care.

Anyway, Kahu had his hands full. His dancer, in full tutu and pointe shoes ensemble, was sitting in his lap, whispering something into his ear.

It was all-in-all quite revolting.

Connor shifted his attention back to the couple across the room again, inexplicably drawn once more. He didn't want to look, but he couldn't seem to help himself.

Victoria's back was toward the room as she faced Raphael, bracing herself with one hand on the arm of his chair. He had his hand on her outstretched forearm and was slowly stroking it up and down in a slow, sensual motion.

The fury inside Connor turned over, a dragon rousing from sleep.

He should go over there right now. Pull her away. Take her somewhere quiet and private where they could talk without that bastard hanging around.

Put her down on her knees. Teach her a goddamned lesson...

He blinked, both disturbed and aroused by the sudden thought. No. No, that wasn't part of it. He couldn't think like that, couldn't afford to. He had to remain in control at all times, it was the bedrock of his existence and had been since he was eighteen.

Across the room, Victoria shifted her position and turned her head to glance over her shoulder. Briefly meeting his gaze. As she did so,

Raphael's arm slid around her waist, his hand settling in the small of her back.

Fucking prick.

Connor tried to moderate his language when he could but sometimes… Christ, his anger was going to choke him if he wasn't careful. If he couldn't get a handle on it.

He had to do something. He had to stop this somehow.

"Not here," Lily was saying. "Are you fucking crazy?"

"I'd be here," Kahu murmured. "And you know I'd kill anyone who tried to touch you."

"That's very reassuring."

"I want to show you off. I want everyone to know how beautiful you are. They'll want you and yet they'll never be able to have you. Because you're mine."

There was a flicker in Victoria's dark eyes as she looked away from him, and Connor could have sworn it was satisfaction.

The woman wanted to make him angry. Wanted to push him. Insanity. Did she really understand what kind of monster she was baiting? No, of course, she didn't. She had no idea. He'd never told her.

"I don't know how you make it sound so bloody romantic," Lily went on quietly. "But you do."

"It's a gift," Kahu replied, a smug note in his voice. "For me, ballerina? I'd get off on it. And I think you might too."

"Pervert."

"Of course. I'm a pervert from way back."

Bright laughter in the air. "Okay. Maybe you're right. Lucky for you I've had a margarita or five so I'm good with it."

The loss of Victoria's attention was like a break in his air supply.

Jesus. That did it. He either left and went home, and calmed the hell down. Or he went over there and…

Lily slid from Kahu's lap, the movement blocking his view of Victoria and Raphael. His hands tightened on the arms of his chair in preparation for pushing himself out of it.

Until, without any fanfare at all, Lily pulled down her tutu and stepped out of it.

Connor stilled in shock.

Because she was naked but for her pointe shoes.

Conversations began to fall silent as Lily moved unhurriedly into the clear space in the center of the room. Then, as if she'd been practicing it for months, began to fall in step with the music.

Connor's body was tight and he realized he was almost sitting up, ready to go and grab her. Cover the lithe muscularity of her naked body with something. Anything. He looked sharply at Kahu, but the other man was sitting back in his chair, completely at ease. He was even smiling as he watched his lovely girl dance naked in front of a whole crowd of strangers.

Christ, he could *not* be happy with her parading about like that, could he?

But Lily wasn't looking at anyone other than Kahu. As if there was no one but them in the entire room.

Connor felt his heart constrict. There was something tender about the look Lily and Kahu shared, something intensely private that shut out the room and everyone in it.

For some strange reason, he found himself helplessly glancing back over at Victoria.

To find her looking back at him.

He couldn't have explained the expression in her eyes. Or the emotion clenched like a fist in his chest. Regret. Sorrow. Pain. A thousand different things. All the emotions he told himself he didn't feel.

Then she looked back at Lily dancing in the center of the room, her expression smoothing over like a wave smoothing the sand, washing away any signs of disturbance.

But Connor found he couldn't look away from her, his heartbeat sounding loud in his head.

And as Lily danced, he knew one thing. He wanted Victoria to look at him the way Lily looked at Kahu. As if he was the only person in the room. As if nothing existed for her but him.

He didn't care what it took, what he had to do to make that happen.

He'd do it.

And then he'd walk away.

Chapter Four

Victoria didn't dare look at Connor again but she could feel his gaze still on her, precise and focused as if he was aiming a gun and she was his target.

She could almost feel his anger like a physical force pushing at her. It was unnerving and yet exhilarating at the same time, because she'd never gotten a response like this from him before. At least never one this intense. And that thrilled her.

The unnerving part was wondering what he was going to do about it. And he would do something about it, of that she was certain. He'd never been a passive kind of man. Hopefully it would be something along the lines of signing those divorce papers so he wouldn't have to see her again.

That's not what you want…

Victoria shook away the insidious thought. It was exactly what she wanted. *Exactly.*

She kept her gaze on Lily, who was dancing in the middle of the room as if she wasn't completely naked. A proud, strong, startling sensual figure.

Victoria had felt uncomfortable watching her at first, like she was viewing something she shouldn't. But Lily hadn't seemed ashamed of being nude. Or worried about people seeing her. In fact, she almost seemed to encourage it with her high kicks, small leaps and graceful turns. She was smiling too, her small, vivid face bright with pleasure. In fact, if anything it was the glances she exchanged with Kahu that were the most exposing. The deep emotion between the two of them was an almost palpable force.

She'd seen it before between Eleanor and Luc too, and had often wondered if she was missing out on something with Connor. Because she didn't have that kind of connection with him. Theirs was a meeting of minds, not bodies.

And not even that, some would say.

Her jaw firmed and she ignored the acid bite of disappointment and regret. Their marriage had been her choice and she couldn't regret that now.

Abruptly Kahu pushed himself out of the armchair as Lily finished a turn. In the dim light of the bar, the sweat burnishing her skin made her seem otherworldly. A beautiful fairy creature.

Kahu said nothing as he came toward her and she made no protest as he scooped her up into his arms, holding her against his chest. Silence reigned as Kahu strode out and continued to do so after he'd gone.

"No prizes for guessing where they're going," Raphael said in her ear.

His breath was warm and she couldn't hold back the shiver as it whispered over her skin. "I guess not downstairs for another drink."

"Oh, I think not." His hand slid down her arm, the gentle caress awakening every nerve ending.

Slowly people began to leave the room, either in search of new entertainment or in search of somewhere more private. More than a few had paired off, the effect of Lily's dance obvious in the way they were looking at each other.

Victoria found her breathing was short, her heartbeat fast.

Connor hadn't moved. She could feel the weight of his stare like the pressure of a storm front pressing down on her.

"You want to stop this?" Raphael murmured. "Or do you want to take it further?"

She swallowed. The logical thing would be to stop this. To get up and go over to Connor and tell him she wanted his signature on those papers and she wanted it by yesterday. Surely he was angry enough to do it by now?

Slowly, she turned her head and glanced across the room again.

There was lightning in his eyes, an intense, furious heat that made something inside her catch fire.

She took an unsteady breath. Was he waiting for her to come to him? Was he expecting her to? Well, if he did, he was out of luck. She wasn't going to be the one to move first. To come to him. She'd already had to do that at the Law Society because of his damn recalcitrance with the papers.

Screw him. This time he would be the one to come to her.

"I want to take it further," she said, trying to keep her voice level, holding Connor's fierce stare with her own.

"You sure?"

"Yes."

"Get in my lap then."

She didn't allow herself to think. Thinking would mean hesitating and she couldn't hesitate because if she did, she'd probably never be able to go through with it.

Getting up out of her armchair, she moved over to the one Raphael was sitting in, then turned around and lowered herself into his lap. His hands rested on her hips as he guided her down, settling her with her head on his shoulder, her legs between his.

"Keep looking at him," he said quietly in her ear. "Don't be afraid."

But she wasn't afraid. Or at least, the reason she was shaking wasn't solely to do with fear. Yes, she'd never done this before, never sat in the lap of a man she barely knew. In a dress that if she moved her leg just little would show the entire world she wasn't wearing anything underneath it. And yes, the thought of that even a couple of days ago would have had her laughing incredulously.

But she also felt...excited in a way she hadn't for years. An intense, visceral thrill that really had nothing to do with the man sitting behind her and everything to do with the man sitting across from her.

Watching her with his eyes full of storms and thunderclouds. Lightning bolts.

He was so still, his long, lean figure absolutely motionless. A furiously angry predator waiting for the kill. His tie was undone at the throat, revealing tanned skin and she couldn't seem to drag her gaze from him.

Raphael shifted her so the split in her dress was open to the hip, revealing almost her entire side. Then his hand came to rest gently on her bare thigh. The touch was like an ember on her skin, burning her and she couldn't stop the sharp intake of breath that escaped her.

"Okay?" Raphael whispered.

"Yes," she croaked.

But she wasn't really. Her skin felt hot, her heart racing, a flood of intense desire gripping her so tight she could hardly breathe.

Connor was like a man turned to stone. But she saw the way his fingers dug into the arms of his chair, knuckles white. As if he was barely holding himself back from getting up and coming over to where she sat. And the look on his face... His jaw was tight, his long, beautiful mouth hard, his eyes glittering with restrained fury.

Intense satisfaction bloomed inside her, mixing with the fear and the desire to become something hot, volatile.

What the hell are you doing? With this complete stranger? You should stop this right now. Before you go too far.

Yet she knew wasn't going to. Something had her in its grip, something powerful. A drive that seemed to come from a place inside herself she hadn't known existed. A wild part of her soul she'd always wanted to explore and yet never had the guts to do so.

A drive fuelled by the expression on Connor's face. By his fury and the undeniable heat in his eyes. And by the fact that he wasn't hiding either of those things. He felt them. And they were both directed at her.

She shouldn't be glorying in his reaction. And she definitely shouldn't want to push him even further.

Yet she felt both of those things.

"More," she said thickly and she wasn't quite sure whom she said it to. Connor or Raphael. Either way, it didn't matter as long as one of them did something.

The hand on her hip moved, sliding under the split of her dress to the soft, sensitive skin of her inner thigh. The breath caught in her throat but he didn't go any further, his thumb beginning to stroke her back and forth.

Victoria shivered helplessly.

And something snapped in Connor's gaze.

He got up out of his chair in a sharp, fluid motion and strode over to the door. Then he looked around the room, at the small number of people still sitting around.

"Out," he ordered.

It was his courtroom voice, strong, deep and full of authority. And everyone slowly began getting to their feet and making for the door like good courtiers before a king.

Within a minute the room was empty apart from her and Raphael.

Connor slammed the door shut. Then he turned and looked at her, and what little breath she had left rushed out of her.

The cold, passionless man she knew from her marriage was gone. In his place was the courtroom tiger, hungry for a victory. For a kill. He began to stalk toward her, focused, intent, fierce. His fury a honed blade she could feel the sharp edge of as he came nearer and nearer.

Her mouth was dry as a desert, her heartbeat rocketing out of control.

Fear curled inside her, not that he'd hurt her—he'd always abhorred violence of any kind—but a different kind of fear she couldn't name. A fear inextricably linked with the pulse of desire throbbing between her thighs.

How had it got to this? Sitting in another man's lap while her husband stalked toward her like a hungry predator?

You like it…

Yes, and perhaps that's why she was afraid.

Connor came closer, his gaze fixed on her. She tensed, her breath thick in her throat.

Raphael didn't move, his body beneath hers completely relaxed. His thumb continued to move on her thigh in a gentle stroke and she wanted to tell him to stop, that perhaps she'd gone too far. But she couldn't speak.

Connor came to a stop right in front of the armchair. He didn't look at Raphael, every ounce of his furious attention focused on her.

Her whole body tensed even further, her fingers digging into the black velvet of the arms of the chair. She tried to keep her expression neutral, to not let any of her fear or her arousal show. She didn't want to give him the satisfaction of knowing he got to her. This was going to be her victory, not his.

"You've been using him to push me all night, Victoria," Connor said, in a low hard voice. "Now it's my turn."

She didn't really understand what he was talking about until his sharp gaze flicked to the man behind her. "You okay with this?"

"Oh, I think so." Raphael's voice was soft and uninflected.

God. So he was going to include Raphael as well. Her whole body tightened.

Connor's gaze dropped back to meet hers. "This is my show from now on," he said quietly, roughly. "Hold her knees apart."

Raphael didn't speak, but he shifted, his hands moving to slide along her thighs and grip her knees, easing them apart. And holding them there.

She sucked in a ragged breath, keeping her gaze on Connor's.

He came closer, standing right in front of the armchair, staring down at her. "You want to push me, Victoria? Make me angry? Is that what you've been trying to do?"

"I just want you to sign the damn papers." Her voice was much thicker than she wanted it to be and slightly shaky.

"And using this man will make me do that?"

Behind her, Raphael was silent. Clearly he understood this actually had nothing to do with him.

"Why not?" she said. "I had to do something."

Connor put his hand on the side of the armchair, near her head, and totally ignoring Raphael, slowly leaned in. "And how far were you going to go? Were you going to fuck him in front of me?"

He almost never swore and there was something about the way he said the word that hit her like a quarrel from a crossbow. A heavy, solid blow, echoing through her.

She could barely breathe, achingly conscious of Raphael's hands on her, his fingers pressing against the sensitive skin on the inside of her knees. Of how open she was beneath her dress. Of the dull ache of need becoming sharper, more intense.

Connor was so close, his mouth right there. Oh God, how long had it been since she'd been that near to him? Close enough to smell the familiar scent of his aftershave, a fresh clean scent that always reminded her of the ocean. To feel the seductive heat of his body.

She hadn't been able to bear being near him for a long time, so close to what she wanted and yet knowing she'd never be able to have it. And yet now…

She swallowed, staring back into the deep, intense blue of his eyes. Meeting his challenge. Answering it. "Would it have made you angry?"

He didn't blink. "Yes."

"Then maybe I would have."

A dense, impossible silence fell. And it was only through sheer force of will that she managed to hold his gaze. It was like looking into the sun. She was almost blinded.

Then he looked down and with his free hand casually flipped aside the silk of her dress along the side-split, baring her to the waist.

Victoria sank her teeth into her lip, holding in the short, shocked sound that threatened to escape as all her muscles locked. Raphael's hands were firm against her flesh, keeping her knees apart. She could feel him beneath her, hot, solid muscle, his scent, in contrast to Connor's, spicy and musky. Not at all unpleasant. He was also hard.

Connor raised his head, looking into her eyes again. "I'm going to give you a choice, Victoria. You can leave, walk out the door now and we can pretend this never happened. Or you stay and show me just how far you're prepared to go to get those papers signed."

She swallowed. "So if I choose not to do this then you won't sign the papers? Is that what you're saying?"

His gaze didn't even flicker. "Yes."

"You manipulative bastard."

"That's interesting coming from the woman in no panties, who's been playing around with another man purely to get back at me."

Her heartbeat was loud in her head, getting faster and faster. She could feel her own anger beginning to rise too, and along with it, the insistent desire. "You can't force me to do anything I don't want to do."

"Neither can you." He put his hand on her thigh, his fingers along her sensitive flesh. "I don't want to sign those papers just yet and I don't like being manipulated into it."

She began to tremble as his fingers moved higher. "And I don't like you refusing to do something entirely reasonable for no reason at all."

"I have a reason." His fingers moved even higher, his gaze burning into hers. "But I'm not going to tell you until you make a decision."

Her body ached, desire and fear clawing up inside her. But she wasn't going to give in. Not yet. "It's not much of a choice," she said through gritted teeth.

"You don't need me to sign those papers in order to leave, Victoria. Nothing is making you stay apart from sheer bloody-mindedness." His deep, rich voice paused. "Unless there *is* something else you're hoping for."

She tried to take a breath and failed. "What?"

His hand moved and she felt the lightest brush of his fingers against her sex. It was only a bare touch but she felt it like he'd trailed a lit match over her skin, leaving her burning, on fire. Instinctively she tried to close her legs but Raphael's fingers tightened, holding her open.

It was a slip. A mistake. Connor's eyes glittered. "Ah, I thought so.

You want me. You want this." And his hand moved between her thighs in another light touch, his fingers beginning to trace the outline of her sex in a slow, lazy movement.

He'd never touched her like this before, purely for the pleasure of it. And she couldn't stop the sound that escaped her this time, a choked gasp as a vicious kind of need began to twist inside her. "I don't...I don't want you," she forced out, her voice ragged.

He leaned in closer. "Tell me to stop then." His fingers moved higher, finding her clit, circling gently, maddeningly.

She wanted to say it, to not give away so much to him. But she couldn't bring herself to get the word out. Because he was right. She wanted him. His dark hunger and his intensity, all the things he'd denied her for too many years.

All the things that burned in his eyes right now.

"I'm s-staying," she said hoarsely. Not an admission, yet not a denial either.

He said nothing for a moment, studying her, his fingers moving in slow, easy circles. "You're wet, Victoria. I can feel it. Is that me or him?"

Him. Raphael. Who was still and silent behind her, keeping her legs apart. God, she'd almost forgotten he was there. She wanted to say it was Raphael, just to push Connor more.

But of course that would be a lie.

Connor's fingers eased lower, his touch on her slick flesh unhurried, as if he had all the time in the world. He looked down at what he was doing and she couldn't seem to stop shaking, the look on his face taut with desire.

This was not the man she married. The man with whom she'd last had perfunctory sex over eighteen months ago. Whose expression had remained shuttered and closed afterwards as he'd given her a dry kiss on the cheek. Leaving her with an aching sense of loss.

No, this was not that man. This was someone else.

"You," she breathed, unable to help herself.

His gaze flicked up, meeting hers. And there was fire in it. And a steely determination that made her tremble even harder.

He took his fingers away, easing back from her and she almost protested, her body tensing, aching at the loss. "Make her come," he ordered softly to the man behind her. "If she wants it from me, she's going to have to earn it."

He saw the anger flare deep in Victoria's dark eyes. And felt the savage twist of his own satisfaction. He'd made her make a mistake. Because he was betting she'd been desperate to keep the fact she wanted him hidden. And yet he'd gotten it out of her, forced her to say it.

His fury began to abate, becoming sharper, more precise.

He didn't look at the man sitting behind her, the guy was almost irrelevant now because what mattered was that she wanted him. And he wasn't going to let her have him.

If she wanted pleasure, she'd have it on his say so and only given by someone else. Because when he finally gave it to her, he wanted her desperate for it. He wanted her begging.

Victoria was panting, her legs held spread and open by Raphael's hands. Her dress pulled tight over her full breasts, the fabric outlining the hard press of her nipples. Black curls cascaded over one shoulder and there were black curls too between her thighs. She was deeply flushed, her mouth full and red, lips parted.

He couldn't stop looking at her.

Over the years he'd tried not to give in to the erotic fantasies that used to invade his dreams. Fantasies about her on her knees, begging him to fuck her. Do anything to her. Anything at all. Fantasies where she looked at him the way Lily had looked at Kahu, and he'd taken her over and over again, hard and rough, giving in to the desire for her that continued to haunt him.

Eventually he'd stopped dreaming about her, but it didn't stop those images from flashing in his head every time he made love to her. They'd made sex so difficult he'd felt nothing but relief when she'd started pulling away from him, sex becoming rarer and rarer between them.

It had been easier that way. Better no sex at all than for him to be at the mercy of his desires. He'd seen firsthand the consequences of that. In other people. And in himself. He even had the reminder inked into his skin so he never forgot.

But perhaps that approach had been a mistake. Perhaps it was better to purge himself of his fury and his hunger once and for all.

His gaze dropped and he let himself look between her thighs, where the folds of her pussy glistened in the dim light of the bar. All wet and open. For him.

Well, she wasn't the only one. He was hard, aching for her, but he wasn't going to give in yet. Not until he got what he wanted from her.

Raphael's hands were moving, sliding up her thigh, but then she said, "Stop." The hands stopped.

Connor looked at her, watching the dark flame burn in her eyes. "Scared?"

But it wasn't fear coloring her cheeks. "No," she snapped. Her head turned slightly. "Do you have a condom, Raphael?"

The other man flashed him a look because it was clear where this was headed.

The blood in his veins began to pound, his breathing accelerating. So she was going to do it. She was going to fuck this guy right in front of him. Pushing him, right to the last.

Well, she wasn't the only one who could push.

He gave Raphael a brief nod.

"Of course," the other man said. "I always have a condom, darling."

Victoria's dark gaze returned to Connor's, full of challenge and fire. "Good. If you're going to make me come, I'd really prefer it if you were inside me."

The atmosphere, already thick and charged, became electric.

Was she expecting him to protest? To lose his temper entirely and storm from the room? No, she wasn't. She was expecting him to stop it. She was expecting him to grab her and fuck her himself.

That was too damn bad. Because he wasn't going to. At least, not yet.

So he said nothing, only watching her as Raphael shifted behind her, putting his hands on her hips and easing her forward. Victoria didn't look to see what he was doing, her gaze firmly on Connor's.

"Does this bother you?" Her voice was soft, a taunting note in it. "Knowing I'm going to have another man inside me?"

Raphael took something out of his pocket, a wallet. He extracted a packet from it.

"Say it properly, Victoria," Connor murmured, watching the color ebb and flow in her cheeks. "You're going to have another man fuck you." And he could see also the effect the word had on her, the faint flicker of her gaze. "What's the matter? Are you going to back out? After I've gotten your pussy good and ready for him?"

Another flicker, her pupils dilating, a soft hitch in her breathing. Oh she liked that, did she? She liked having him say those filthy words to her. Words they'd never, ever said to each other before.

The sound of a zipper being drawn down was loud in the room, the crackle of foil following it. Her knuckles were white on the arms of the chair.

Jesus. Did she really want this?

He moved closer to the chair, the scent of musk and sex already heavy in the air. Reaching out, he took her chin in his hand, forcing her head back, looking down into her wide, black eyes. "You don't have to do this," he said softly.

She didn't move, but he could see the brief gleam of triumph in her gaze. "Jealous, Connor?"

"You're afraid."

A flicker of shock crossed her face then it was gone. "Not of this. Do it, Raphael."

Connor didn't release her chin, watching her, and she didn't look away as the other man lifted her slightly, positioning himself. Then her eyes widened, a soft sound escaping her as she was lowered again and Connor couldn't help looking down as the other man's cock pushed into her, the soft, wet folds, her pussy spreading to accommodate him.

It was the most erotic sight he'd ever seen in his life.

Raphael gave a soft grunt, one arm sliding around her waist, holding her in position.

"Wait," Connor ordered. He was going to be in charge of this, not her. Tightening his grip on her chin, he said, "Keep your eyes on me, Victoria. Only on me."

She was shaking, that cool, shuttered gaze of hers now wide and open. Staring at him.

"Fuck her, Raphael," he said softly. "But take it slowly because I've changed my mind. I don't want you to make her come. I want to do it."

She hadn't meant to take it this far, she really hadn't. But he'd forced the admission from her and she'd been so damn angry. She hadn't wanted him to know. She'd never wanted him to know. And now he did so she had to do something.

But she couldn't remember now what she'd even been trying to prove because she was sitting in this chair, and Raphael was inside her. And Connor had her chin in his hand, forcing her to look into his blazing blue eyes, where there was nothing but fury and heat.

And she was shaking with desire.

But he was right, she was also afraid. Afraid of the part of herself that had made her do this. That had pushed and pushed, gotten so carried away she was letting another man have sex with her while her husband watched.

Have sex? Say it, Victoria. You're letting another man fuck you…

Her mouth opened but nothing came out as Raphael's arm tightened around her waist. As his hips flexed and he thrust, his breath harsh in her ear. She gasped, feeling the push of his cock inside and the helpless movement of her own body meeting it.

"You like that, don't you, dirty girl?" Connor's voice was rough and soft as frayed velvet, his grip on her chin hard. "You like having him fucking you while I watch."

Oh God. Those words. They made her feel so bad. So wrong. So filthy. It was the most intense pleasure she'd ever experienced in her entire life.

His grip on her chin firmed as Raphael thrust again, as she let out another gasp. "That's right, Victoria. Enjoy his cock while you can." His thumb ran across her lower lip, tracing the soft curve of it, making her shiver. "Because that's all you're going to get of it."

The touch of his thumb was so light it was unbearable. The blazing heat in his eyes blinding. And yet she couldn't look away. The pleasure was gathering inside her, a dense, hard knot of sensation.

She began to pant, her world narrowing to the blue of Connor's eyes, to the flex of Raphael's hips and the slide of him inside her, driving her further and further to the edge.

Connor's thumb settled against her mouth and then pushed inside. The salty taste of his skin flooded her, adding to the intensity of the sensations. "Suck it, dirty girl," he whispered. "Suck it like it's my cock. And if you do it well enough, maybe I'll let you come."

Perhaps she had gone too far, a part of her desperate to turn back. But now it was too late and she knew it. She'd opened the box and let out the darkness, and there was no way she could put it back in again.

Perhaps you don't even want to.

She closed her mouth on Connor's thumb, swirling her tongue around him. And she licked him, sucked him. Did exactly what she was told, watching as the desire in his gaze burned brighter, fiercer. God, she wasn't the only one who was desperate.

Raphael's thrusts became faster, the slide of his cock inside her a delicious friction that had her forgetting she was supposed to be hiding her pleasure. Restraining her desire. Had her forgetting who she was entirely.

She gave a strangled moan, lifting her hands to touch the man standing in front of her, wanting him helplessly.

"Oh, no you don't," Connor said softly. "Hold her hands down."

And Raphael's fingers were there, wrapping around her wrists, gently pulling her hands down onto the arms of the chair and keeping them there.

She took a ragged breath, the sense of restraint both exciting and maddening. In retaliation she closed her teeth around Connor's thumb, watching with intense satisfaction as the look in his eyes flared.

"Harder," he growled. "Fuck her harder."

Raphael's body flexed under hers, his fingers tight on her wrists as he thrust up into her in short, hard movements.

Everything began to dissolve around the edges, including all her plans and good intentions. There was only this. Only the pleasure Connor was directing. Only the release that was so near and yet so damn far away.

She moaned, Raphael's ragged breathing against her ear as he turned his face into her hair.

"What do you need to do, dirty girl?" Connor murmured. He took his thumb out of her mouth, slicking it over her lower lip, making it wet. "I want to hear you say it."

"I…" She could barely speak. "I need to… come."

"And what do you say?"

"P-please."

"Please what?"

"Please, Connor."

"Beg me, dirty girl. Beg me and I might let you."

And the words came out whether she wanted them to or not. "Please, Connor. Oh, please. Please let me come."

A savage kind of smile turned his mouth. "Good. That's exactly what I wanted to hear."

He reached down between her thighs with his other hand and found her clit. Brushed his thumb over it once, twice.

Raw lightning ignited as the orgasm rushed over her, Connor's mouth covering hers. Swallowing her choked scream and the series of desperate cries that followed it as she rode out the wave of unbelievable pleasure.

Raphael let go of her hands, one arm sliding around her waist and holding her still as he thrust hard and deep, chasing his own release, his sharp groan echoing as he found it.

Victoria closed her eyes, aware only of Connor's mouth, tasting him in the bright darkness behind her lids, whisky and heat, and an unexpected sweetness. His fingers wound into her hair, cradling her head as the kiss went on and on. As she lost herself in it.

He'd never kissed her like this before, with raw passion and heat, his tongue exploring, caressing. Their kisses had always been perfunctory, dutiful almost. Kisses that had left her empty and hollow.

But this was nothing like that. This kiss had her shaking, her already satisfied body gathering itself into desire with shocking speed.

She put her hands on his shoulders, leaning forward into him.

This was what she wanted. What she had always wanted. More of this, more of him.

And she wasn't going to be satisfied anymore with anything less.

Chapter Five

Her hair was the softest thing he'd ever touched and she tasted of the wine she'd been drinking and of desperation. Of pure, passionate sex. And all he could think of was it was a bloody good thing he hadn't ever kissed her like this before because now he'd started, he wasn't sure if he'd be able to stop.

But he had to stop. He had a proposal to put to her and if he wanted her agreement, he had to keep something back.

Connor lifted his head, breaking the kiss.

Victoria was looking up at him, a deep flush staining her smooth olive skin, her lips wet and full. Her eyes were hazy with desire, and for a second he just wanted to keep looking at her like this, wanted to imprint on his memory the image of Victoria, hot for him.

Then there was a movement behind her and he remembered suddenly it wasn't just the two of them in the room.

"Move for me, sweetheart," Raphael said softly, an edge of roughness in his voice.

Victoria blinked as if she too, had forgotten he was there.

Connor let her go, straightening and stepping back to give them some space.

A distant part of himself was appalled at his own behavior. That he'd encouraged another man to fuck his wife and had given him instructions on how to do it into the bargain, was not in any way normal behavior for him. In fact, it was just the kind of behavior he'd always loathed and been disgusted by. Yet he'd given in to his darker self and done it anyway.

He should be disgusted at himself. But he wasn't. In fact, he was hard, aching to sink his cock into her, make her scream the way she'd screamed just now.

As Victoria slid from Raphael's lap, smoothing down her dress with shaking hands, he toyed briefly with the idea of getting her to relieve that ache immediately. Putting her on her knees, getting her to suck him off maybe.

But no, he'd decided he was going to hold back, wasn't he? And after all, he had the control now and he wanted to keep it.

Raphael had moved to the bar, leaning over it to get rid of the condom in the trash while Victoria stood near the armchair, still smoothing non-existent wrinkles from her dress. She didn't look at Connor, the expression on her face utterly impassive. But he could take a guess at what she was feeling anyway. Embarrassed, unsure. Awkward. And understandably. It wasn't like either of them had done anything like this before.

As Raphael turned from the bar and walked over to where Victoria stood, Connor tensed. "You can't kiss her," he said harshly, unable to help himself. "Only I get to do that."

The other man didn't take offense. He reached out and took Victoria's hand instead, raising an eyebrow at Connor. "This okay?" There was no challenge in the words, only a simple question.

The tension inside him loosened. Clearly the guy understood what was happening here and was fine with it. He nodded and Raphael raised Victoria's hand to his lips in an old-fashioned courtly gesture. She lifted her chin in response, her mouth relaxing into an almost-smile. Raphael released her. "Thank you," he said and then glanced at Connor, including him too. There was a complicated expression on his face, one Connor couldn't interpret, but he thought he saw respect in it and something like a warning.

He didn't reply, only gave the other man another curt nod, and remained silent as Raphael turned and left the room, closing the door behind him.

The silence lengthened, became heavy with the weight of what had just happened.

Victoria bent to grab the purse she'd put down beside her chair and straightened. The passionate woman he'd kissed before was gone, to be replaced by the cool, reserved lawyer. "Well?" Her voice was crisp and brittle. "Since I screwed someone in front of you, does this mean I get my divorce?"

And abruptly the anger was back, coiling inside him like a snake. He was still hard, he was still hungry and she was looking at him as if nothing at all had changed.

"No," he said. "It means you get to listen to my proposal."

"I hardly think that's—"

"Shut up and listen."

Fire glinted in her eyes, but she didn't speak. Good choice.

He closed the distance between them, wanting to get up in her face again, get close, watch that reserve crumble like it had while she was in the armchair, while he was directing her pleasure.

She didn't move, but her jaw hardened, her mouth in a tight line as he came closer.

He stopped, inches away, looking down into her face. The scent of sex was still in the air, intensifying the ache in his groin. He ignored it. "I will sign those papers. But only on one condition."

"Oh? And what's that?"

"I want you for one week and one week only. In my bed."

Something flickered in her gaze, immediately masked. "Sex, you mean?"

"Yes, that's exactly what I mean."

"Why? When you've never shown the slightest bit of interest in sex with me before?"

He should give her the truth. Tell her he'd wanted her since the day he'd first seen her. But he wouldn't. Because that would lead to other questions, other truths he wasn't prepared to give to anyone, let alone her.

"That was then," he said. "This is now. And now what I want is you."

"Really?" Her mouth twisted. "You'll forgive me if I find that a little hard to believe."

He didn't think, reaching out and closing his fingers around the slender bones of her wrist. Pulling her hand down and pressing it to the front of his suit trousers, where his damn hard-on was still going strong. "Do you believe me now?"

Her gaze flicked down to where he was holding her hand, her mouth opening slightly. And he heard her breath catch. The heat from her palm was sweet agony, but he didn't release her wrist, keeping her hand there.

A tense, silent second passed.

"Well?" he demanded. "Say it, Victoria."

"Yes," she said after a moment, her voice thick. "I believe you."

"Then what's your answer?"

Her attention stayed on her hand, slim fingers spread on the black wool of his trousers. "If all you want is sex, why can't you find someone else? Why do you need me?"

Another good question. But this wasn't purely about sex and it never had been. It was about a desire that had been simmering away for years, kept hidden, kept secret, that he was only now allowing to be set free. An intense, physical desire which had always been for her and only for her.

Oh, he'd looked at other women over the years. And he'd felt some vague twinges of attraction for them. But not in the way he felt for Victoria. Not with such intensity and insistence. Marrying her had been the wrong thing to do, yet he'd done it anyway, not wanting to let her go.

Yeah, and your marriage became an agony.

Maybe it had been. Which made now the perfect time to put it behind them once and for all.

"Because I don't want anyone else," he said. "I want you. Take it or leave it."

Her fingers pressed against him unexpectedly, the breath catching in his throat at the touch. Then she looked up at him, her eyes dark. "And if I say no?"

"You don't get your divorce."

"Neither do you."

"I can live with that."

She looked away and he felt her wrist tense against his fingers. He didn't release her. He would have this. He would.

"You bastard." Her voice was soft.

"Does that mean you're going to lie again? Tell me you don't want me?"

"Let me go."

"No. You can feel what you do to me, Victoria. And I saw what I did to you. Don't tell me you don't find the thought of a week in my bed even a little bit intriguing."

"Intriguing is not the way I'd describe our sex life for the past five years."

He stilled, staring down into her face, studying her expression. Because that almost sounded like...regret.

He'd never had one sign from her she wanted him physically, not one. Until tonight. And that lack of interest had been one of the reasons he'd decided to marry her. It made her safe. And if she'd shown she wanted him, he would have broken it off to protect both of them.

But she hadn't. And so he'd married her. And in the whole five years of that marriage, they'd never spoken about their brief, passionless couplings. Never discussed them. Because there wasn't any reason to. He'd assumed both of them were happy with the way things were.

Yet judging from the look on her face, perhaps that wasn't the case after all. Did he actually want to know? No, perhaps not yet.

"I thought what happened just now was fairly intriguing," he said. "Or did you fake that orgasm?"

Something flashed in her eyes. "Would you even be able to tell if I did?"

His free hand came out before he could stop it, taking her chin between his fingers, holding her fast. In the silence of the room, he could hear her indrawn breath. "I would know, Victoria," he said, not bothering to hide the steel in his voice. "Believe me, I would know."

The fierce gleam in her eyes didn't lessen. She stared up at him for a long moment, making no move to escape his grasp. And he felt the desire inside him turn over and over, until he was only holding onto his control by a bare thread. He'd never seen this woman either, this challenging, confronting woman.

Christ, he was *this* close to losing it.

"One week," she said abruptly. "But not the kind of sex we've been having for the past five years. I want more than that, so if you can't give it to me, then I guess I'll have to be stuck with no divorce."

Satisfaction rolled through him and he let it show on his face. "We will not be having that kind of sex, don't worry." Moving his thumb, he brushed it across her mouth in a subtle reminder and she shivered. "The kind of sex we'll be having is how I want. When I want. Anywhere I want. You will not get a say."

Again her eyes glinted, anger moving in the depths like a deep ocean current. Her lips parted against his thumb. "That doesn't sound like I'd get anything from it."

"You can really say that? After you came so beautifully for me?"

"If you want to have sex with me, Connor, you can just do so now and get it over with."

He pressed his thumb a little harder against the softness of her lower lip. "But that's the thing, Victoria. I don't want to just have sex with you. I want to fuck you. Repeatedly."

A blush stained her cheeks and her lashes lowered, hiding her gaze. And he knew he had her. She wouldn't refuse.

Slowly, he pushed his thumb into her mouth, feeling heat and wetness against his skin, watching as her red lips closed around it. A bad thing to do when he was so close to the edge, but he couldn't help himself. He wanted to give her a reminder before he walked away.

"The only down side for you," he went on softly, "is that if you want my cock, you're going to have to earn it."

Then abruptly he pulled his thumb from her mouth. Released her wrist.

And turned and walked out of the room without a backward glance.

Come at seven. Wear this. Don't be late.
C.

Victoria put down the note on the table then gazed at the small box that had been delivered to her apartment that morning, along with the note. She wasn't quite sure she wanted to open it and see what was inside.

Nothing good probably.

Or alternatively, something very good...

Her jaw tightened as desire clenched hard inside her. No. Just because she'd done something incredibly illicit last night did *not* mean she wanted to keep on exploring that part of her. Last night was supposed to be a one-off. It wasn't supposed to continue.

God, even thinking about it, Raphael inside her, Connor watching her...

Despite herself, an insistent dark pleasure rolled through her, seductive and hot.

Victoria turned sharply away from the box on the kitchen table and walked a couple of steps to the window, staring out at the view over Auckland's harbor that had attracted her to buy the apartment on the wharf in the first place. The view of the sea with the crescent of the harbor bridge just off to her left, the dark triangle of Rangitoto to the right, smoky and black against the deep blue sky, always calmed her. Centered her. She liked the sea, found it restful. Always had. And yet today, even the sight of the yachts didn't do anything to calm her rapidly beating pulse.

What had she let herself in for with Connor?

After he'd left the room the night before, she'd gone downstairs not quite sure what to do with herself. The party had been still going strong, getting to the extremely raucous part of the evening. She hadn't been able to face rejoining it, deciding to go home instead, deeply unsettled by what had happened in the room upstairs. By what she had done and what she had revealed.

Her only consolation was that Connor, apparently, felt the same. He wanted her. And for some reason, he wanted her badly enough to use the divorce papers as a means to have her.

She should feel pissed off about that and she did. But there was also a traitorous sense of satisfaction that came along with it she found disturbing. She hadn't known how much she'd wanted him to want her until that moment. Which was weak of her. She'd thought she'd gotten over needing that from others years ago, when she'd moved out of home and shifted to Auckland to go to university. But it seemed like she hadn't. Seemed she still wanted acknowledgement from someone.

God, how ridiculous.

She turned back to the table and stared at the box.

Why had she agreed to Connor's demands? Yes, she wanted him to sign those papers, but she didn't need them to start her new life. It wasn't like she would ever marry again in all likelihood, so whether he signed them or not was irrelevant. He was a loose end that needed tying up, nothing more.

Yet, she'd ended up agreeing all the same.

You know why.

Of course she did. It was because that dark part of her wanted more of what Connor had given her the night before. Had wanted to explore those feelings and sensations. Wanted to be bad for him. Be dirty for him.

A shiver went through her. She'd strayed so far from what was right last night and yet it had been…so good. Like she'd been starving for years and the first food to be given to her had been chocolate. Too rich. Decadent. Overwhelming. And yet she had to have more.

Victoria pushed herself away from the window and walked quickly back over to the table. She took the lid off the box and put it down carelessly onto the tabletop. A tissue-wrapped package sat in the middle of the box. She pulled aside the paper, suddenly impatient.

In the middle of the white tissue sat folds of black silk and fine chains. Puzzled, she lifted out the item, trying to see what it was.

The black silk looked to be a pair of tiny black panties. But the chains? She frowned, trying to figure it out. The chains were a complex web attached to a ring that looked like it was supposed to sit over the bellybutton. A center chain ran up from it to attach around another ring, slender and gold, big enough to sit around the neck. There were more chains creating another web across each breast, clearly designed to accentuate rather than hide.

God. So he wanted her to wear that. With presumably nothing on underneath it but the panties.

She looked at the chains in her hands. They glittered in the light from the windows, a delicate golden bronze. The color would suit her skin perfectly and no doubt he'd been aware of that when he'd chosen it from whatever shop he'd gone to. It was a beautiful piece, certainly. But she couldn't wear it, could she?

You had sex with another man in front of Connor. Wearing this will be easy.

Victoria put the lingerie or whatever it was back down into the tissue paper with a decisive movement. She could wear it, but that was a small step on a slippery slope. If she did, then she'd be tacitly allowing Connor to take control of everything, including herself.

Did she really want that?

She left the kitchen and went out into her open-plan lounge area, with the big windows also facing onto the harbor. Her phone was charging on a side table near the couch so she went over to it and took out the cable. Then she pressed the button that would call Connor.

He answered on the second ring. "You got the package?" he asked without any preamble.

The wanton creature inside her shivered at the deep, rich sound of his voice. God, she was insane. "You can't seriously expect me to wear that?" she asked, ignoring the shiver.

"The playsuit? Yes, of course I expect you to wear it."

"Why?"

"Because it's sexy and because you'll look beautiful in it."

The compliment was unexpected, a whisper of warmth moving through her. Damn him. "I don't want to wear it."

He didn't even hesitate. "Then don't bother coming."

"Connor—"

"Where I want. How I want. Whatever I want. That's how it's going to be, Victoria."

She gritted her teeth, trying to ignore the way the warmth began to gather into heat at the hard, flat sound of his voice. "Why does it have to be what you want? What about what I want?"

"You want me. Inside you."

She swallowed, staring down at the carpet, her heart beating uncomfortably fast. *He's right. You do.* "You're being a bastard."

"And you're being a liar."

"I'm not lying!"

"Aren't you? You weren't lying when you told me you wanted me. You weren't lying when you screamed into my mouth when you came." His voice became lower, rougher. "Is it assurances you want, Victoria? You know I won't hurt you, if that's what you're worried about."

Her hands tightened on her phone, the burnished edge of it cutting into her palm. Of course she knew that. But admitting she wanted assurances would mean admitting she was afraid. And she didn't want him to know. Because it wasn't him she was afraid of. It was herself and her desires. Her fear of letting them run free, of taking whatever he wanted to give her. Of wanting it too much. "I'm not worried," she said, trying to keep her voice level. "But this leaves you with a hell of a lot of control and me with none."

There was a pause. "You don't trust me?" There was no inflection in his voice.

A good question. Did she trust him? "I...don't know," she said after a moment, allowing him the hesitation. "Physically, I do but..." She stopped, not wanting to go into it.

He was silent too and the quiet seemed to be full of all the unsaid things between them. And she realized a cold, hard fact: there was no trust between them and perhaps there never had been.

You would have told him about Jessica if there had been.

"Will you trust me with your pleasure then?" Connor asked eventually, breaking the silence. "I would have thought, after last night, you could at least do that."

She swallowed. "You haven't given me much choice."

"Of course you have a choice. You don't have to come to me tonight at all."

"But if I don't, you won't sign the papers."

"No." The word was blunt. Another silence. Then he said, "I want you, Victoria. I want to see you in the playsuit. And I want to make you scream again. That's all I've been thinking about all fucking day." There was a quiet emphasis to the words, an insistence that made her suddenly breathless.

He wanted her. Inexplicably, after five damn years, he wanted her. Did she need anything more?

She took a breath. "Can I tell you to stop?"

"Yes. But I may not."

Another shiver went through her. *You don't want him to.* "I'm not sure I like the sound of that."

"You're afraid, Victoria?"

The bastard. "No," she said and luckily it didn't sound like too much of a lie. "I'm just looking after my own safety."

He didn't say anything immediately, as if he was thinking it through. Then he said, "All right, you say stop and I'll give you five minutes. If you truly don't want it after the five minutes is up, we'll do something else. Otherwise we'll continue. How does that sound?"

Typical lawyer. It was, irritatingly, both fair and logical, and she couldn't work out why the thought of it annoyed her. "Yes, okay," she replied reluctantly. "Where are you planning on doing this then?"

"My house."

His house. Their house. Or at least, it used to be their house. She'd been happy to move out and he'd wanted to keep it. It was a sprawling colonial villa in Herne Bay, on the fringe of the inner city and near the sea. Over the years, the neighborhood had gotten expensive and Connor would have made a fair bit of money if he'd sold it. But for some reason he hadn't.

"Right," she said. "I guess I should be glad it's not some seedy hotel room."

The sound of Connor shifting around came down the phone. "Any more questions?"

"I haven't said yes yet."

He ignored that. "Don't be late," he said and ended the call abruptly.

"Bastard," Victoria said to the empty room. And then, for good measure, "Fucking bastard."

She threw the phone down on the couch, giving in to her temper. God, how she hated his arrogance, his total assurance she'd be there. The way he was using his signature to get her to do what he wanted. And more than anything, the way he was using her desire against her. She wished the part of her that had woken upstairs in the bar last night was still sleeping. Or better yet, wasn't there at all.

But it was. And it wanted what Connor had promised her. Five years of being stifled in a cold marriage had made it hungry, starving for heat and passion. Desperate to see what more there could be. And from him, only from him.

She stared at the offending piece of technology on the couch, debating whether or not she should call up Raphael and maybe ask him for what she wanted. But deep down, she knew she wasn't going to. That would only be out of spite, not because she actually wanted him. She didn't want him. Whether she liked it or not, she wanted Connor.

A sigh escaped her. Perhaps she should call Eleanor, talk it through. Then again, what would be the point? Connor wanted a week and after that, the papers would be signed, her problem solved. She was making a fuss over nothing, over a week of hot sex with her handsome husband.

So why on earth was she making a big deal out of it?

Victoria went back into the kitchen where the little playsuit lay in its tissue paper. She stared at it for a long moment then she reached out and picked it up. Yes, it was very, very pretty.

Turning, she took it through into the bedroom to try it on.

Chapter Six

Connor hadn't been able to concentrate all day. From the moment he'd woken up that morning, hard and aching, all he could think about was Victoria with her legs spread and Raphael's cock in her, screaming out her orgasm into his mouth. He'd never had it so bad, not since he'd been fourteen and one of his father's customers, a prostitute called Candy, had started coming onto him, hoping for free drugs in return for a couple of blowjobs. Being a teenage boy, he'd been obsessed by the idea, finally letting her do it to him one night when his father was out and his mother was safely in bed asleep. And it probably would have been great if his father hadn't come home unexpectedly and discovered what was going on. He'd beaten the poor girl senseless—Damian Blake's usual mode of dealing with people who wanted to pay him with something other than money—and then he'd turned on his son.

Connor had gotten his arm broken for the privilege and had never so much as looked at any of his father's customers after that. Even at school, with girls his own age, he'd kept away from them because it just wasn't worth it. His father was dangerous, unpredictable, and he hadn't wanted to draw anyone else into his shitty life.

So he'd learned to ignore his desires. Pretend they didn't exist and for years, until he'd lost his virginity at eighteen to a pretty student he'd met at law school, that had worked well.

Until last night. Until Victoria.

He'd gotten up that morning and headed straight to an exclusive lingerie store, his head full of plans of what he wanted to do with her when she came over that night. He'd never bought a woman lingerie before, and he'd had visions of her in something pretty and sexy. And then he'd seen the little playsuit with its chains and knew he wouldn't rest until he'd seen her in it.

It was hideously expensive, but he bought it then delivered it himself to her door without going in. He didn't want to be there when she opened it because he wanted this to be her decision. He wanted her to choose him. And perhaps it was a risk, but a part of him was certain that's exactly what she'd choose.

She'd let him take control last night, confessed she wanted him, the look in her eyes flaring every time he'd used dirty language. Every time he'd told her what he wanted from her. Regardless of what she told herself, she wanted this and they both knew it.

She was just pissed at giving up her control, which was understandable. But now he was in charge, he wasn't going to give it up in a hurry. He'd had five years of ignoring the temptation she presented so completely he'd forgotten it existed at all. And had starved himself in the process. Well, he wasn't going to go hungry any longer.

He had a week. He was going to fucking take it.

That afternoon he ditched his plans to get takeout for dinner and, needing something to focus on, decided to cook instead. He quite liked cooking precisely because it got him out of his head, calmed him down, and he didn't often have the chance to do it since he was usually so busy with work.

He should probably have gone over his notes on the Anderson case, but he couldn't concentrate on it, not when he kept thinking about Victoria. So he spent the time looking through his cookbooks, trying to figure out what to cook, trying to remember what foods Victoria liked to eat. Not that he was cooking for her, of course. This was about what he wanted after all. But if the meal was something she liked, then that wouldn't be a bad thing.

Eventually, remembering she'd always seemed partial to a nicely cooked steak, he got a couple out of the freezer. They wouldn't take long to cook which would give them an hour or two to play around first.

Just before seven, Connor went upstairs and had a quick shower, dressing in jeans and a T-shirt, nothing fancy. Then afterwards he prowled around in the lounge, flicking on the TV and channel surfing, trying not to look at the time.

His phone buzzed a couple of times, but it wasn't Victoria. Only a couple of texts from Kahu about the party. There was nothing about a supposed threesome which meant Raphael hadn't said anything. Just as well. Connor would have to have words with him if he had.

But of course checking the texts meant he caught a glimpse of the time. Fifteen minutes after seven. Victoria was late.

Did that mean she wasn't coming?

He was conscious of a sudden, strange sensation in his stomach at the thought. Undeniable disappointment. Which was not at all what he expected.

Flicking the TV off, he chucked the remote down onto the minimalist white coffee table, familiar anger beginning to burn. Jesus, what the hell was he going to do if she didn't turn up? His usual modus operandi would be to ignore it. Tell himself it didn't matter and eat his bloody dinner alone.

But he wasn't sure he'd be able to do that now. He'd promised himself this. And he wanted her. He fucking *wanted* her.

He turned and strode into the hallway, going over to the little console table where he kept his keys and wallet. Time go after her, see where the hell she'd gotten to. Because he wasn't going to be able to ignore her this time.

And then there came a knock on the door and his whole body tensed up with anticipation.

He left his keys and wallet where they were and stalked over to the front door, pulling it open.

Victoria stood on the doorstep. She wore a black trench coat, belted at the waist, and the high, red silk sandals she'd worn the night before. Her hair was loose again, thick black curls like a cloud over her shoulders. She didn't say a word, but there was a certain defiance in her gaze.

Every muscle went tight as he stared at her. She must be wearing what he'd sent her—why else would she be in a coat when she usually favored suits? And her legs were bare. And she definitely wouldn't wear those sandals in the normal scheme of things... Christ. His cock was getting hard already.

"You're late," he said, knowing even as the words left his mouth that it would reveal he'd been impatient.

"Yes," she said coolly. "I'm sorry about that. Couldn't be helped."

Her tone was a challenge all in itself, the look in her dark eyes telling him she was going to give him a battle. And he felt everything in him rise to meet it.

He stepped aside to allow her entry. "Come in."

Her gaze flickered a little at his neutral tone but she entered without hesitation, the heady, drowned magnolia scent of her perfume trailing after her.

She was trying to one-up him by being late, he was certain of it.

Well, she would be wrong.

He closed the door behind him, Victoria already halfway down the hall toward the back of the house where the lounge area was.

"Stop," he ordered, putting every ounce of authority he possessed into the word.

She did so, turning around, one eyebrow arching in cool enquiry. Christ, he wanted that self-possessed, self-contained look off her face.

"You think you can turn up here, late, without an explanation, and not get any comeback?"

Victoria's expression remained entirely neutral. "I'm here, aren't I?"

"And I told you not to be late."

"Really, Connor, I don't know what—"

"Get on your knees."

Her mouth shut, a gleam showing in her dark eyes.

But he wasn't having any of that. "Where I want, how I want, whatever I want. Remember, Victoria? You're here. Which means you made your choice."

For a minute she didn't do anything. Then she shrugged, as if it didn't matter to her one way or the other, and dropped to her knees on the red and blue Persian rug that ran the length of the hallway. "I didn't think it would bother you," she said, shifting around as if trying to get comfortable.

"It did bother me," he said, satisfied as he walked toward her. Finally, there she was. Exactly as he'd fantasized. "It bothered me a lot."

A frown appeared between her brows as he approached, uncertainty in the depths of her eyes. Clearly she hadn't been expecting him to admit it. Well, good. He was sick of pretending he didn't feel it and tonight he wasn't going to.

He stopped directly in front of her. "I told you not to be late. Seven sharp, not quarter past."

"It's only fifteen minutes. I hardly—"

He reached out, gripped her chin and tipped her head back. "I've been waiting for you all day, dirty girl. And I didn't want to wait another fifteen minutes."

The long, graceful column of her throat moved, a flush rising to her cheeks as she stared up at him, the color exquisite in the deep olive of her skin. "I'm not a dirty girl."

"Yes, you are. Tonight you're my dirty girl." He traced her bottom lip with his thumb, a subtle reminder of the night before. "Now, tell me you're sorry and I'll let you suck my cock."

Her mouth opened a little, her eyes darkening, the brown deepening into black. "What if I'm not sorry?"

"Then you don't get to have it."

"I might not want it."

"Really." He released her and reached down to the fly of his jeans. The desire inside him was desperate but he could control it. He wanted this slow, to tease her. To get the truth out of her once and for all. Slowly, he undid the button then took hold of the tab of his zipper.

Her gaze had dropped to his hand, watching his movements. So he didn't rush, dragging down the zipper, feeling the tight fabric part, seeing her mouth open a little more as it did so. Oh yeah, this was what he wanted, her as hungry for him as he was for her.

"Are you sure?" he asked, his voice gone rough. Then he slid his hand down inside his boxers and gripped his cock, making sure she could see the outline through the fabric. "Say you're sorry for being late, Victoria. And you can suck me off. Otherwise I'll get myself off with my hand and you only get to watch."

She looked up at him for a second and their eyes met. And his stomach lurched.

He felt like some part of himself had been stripped away and now she was looking at the man underneath. A man kept hidden for so long Connor had forgotten he was there.

In that moment he knew she could break him. That the power had shifted and now she had it. And all she needed to do was call his bluff. Get up and leave. And if she did, he would break.

He'd allowed himself to want. Too much and too badly. The one thing he could never, ever do…

The moment lengthened, tension crawling through him.

Pull away. Protect yourself.

He should. He really should. And yet he didn't move. Because the expression in her eyes had changed, as if a curtain had been drawn back from a room he'd always wanted to look inside of and now he could see in. There was trepidation there and wonder, and shock. And a desperation to match his own.

She didn't look away, letting him see everything. The other woman behind her cool, collected mask. The woman he'd finally met for the first time up in the bar the night before.

Then she said hoarsely, "I'm sorry I was late, Connor."

And his stomach lurched again, a tension releasing, a wave of some strange emotion he couldn't identify rolling through him. He pushed his fingers into the softness of her hair, clenching them tight, suddenly sick of the ache in his groin. Sick of teasing and sick of holding back.

"Take off your coat," he ordered.

"But you—"

"Don't worry, you'll get what you want. But I need something beautiful to look at."

Her hands lifted to the belt of her trench coat and he saw her fingers were shaking. The emotion sitting in his chest deepened. Fuck, yeah. He liked that she was trembling, that the force of this desire was affecting her as much as it was affecting him. Because he was pretty damn sure his hands would be trembling too if they weren't already occupied.

Victoria pulled her coat off and let it fall on the ground behind her. And Connor let himself look.

His breath hissed, lust becoming more insistent.

She wore the playsuit he'd bought her, along with the black panties and nothing else. And she was the most goddamn beautiful thing he'd ever seen.

The only times they'd gotten naked with each other had been in the dark, those brief, passionless encounters where they'd made love. Or rather, had sex since love had never been part of the equation. And they'd never touched each other's bodies purely for the pleasure of it, or even looked at each other. He'd made certain of that.

But he looked now, his gaze following every line, every curve. She'd lost weight, he was pretty sure, and that made his heart tighten for reasons he didn't want to dwell on. Nevertheless she still had the most gorgeous curves, breast and hip and thigh all gently rounded and eminently strokable. Her skin was deep olive and smooth, a legacy from some Polynesian ancestor, the color contrasting beautifully with the gold chains webbing her body. They glittered in the light, brushing against the hard tips of her nipples.

"Fucking beautiful," he murmured, making no attempt to hide his appreciation. "I knew it would look fantastic on you."

She blushed, but didn't look away. "You promised me something."

"So I did." He tugged on her hair, hearing her breathing catch. Interesting. "Getting impatient, dirty girl?"

"N-no."

He smiled, but not because anything was funny. Because everything was desperate and he liked that. "Open your mouth then. Dirty girls who do what they're told get rewards."

She obeyed without hesitation, her gaze on his.

Connor jerked down his boxers, freeing himself. Then he gripped tight onto her hair and slowly eased his cock into her mouth.

Wet heat engulfed him and he couldn't stop the growl that escaped at the sight of her opening up to take him, red lips against his skin as she closed her mouth around him. Her eyes had gone completely black, glazed with hunger.

"Jesus," he whispered, the blood pumping so hard in his veins she'd probably be able to hear it too.

Her tongue moved, stroking the underside of his shaft, and he bit out another rough curse. If he wasn't careful this was probably going to end way too quickly.

Pushing his other hand into her hair, he held her in place. "Stay still." And then he flexed his hips, pulling out then pushing back in again, taking it slow because he knew she wasn't used to this.

Well, shit, neither are you.

No, Christ, when was the last time he'd had a blowjob? Before they were married…

He looked down at her, into her eyes. She was so familiar to him and yet he'd never had her here before. On her knees with her lips wrapped around his cock, wearing a net of chains showcasing full, beautiful breasts. And black panties barely covering her pussy. That were transparent and through which he could see silky black curls.

Oh…Jesus…

"That feels good," he murmured, pleasure continuing to build inside him. "You like that? You like my cock in your mouth?"

Her throat moved, her gaze never leaving his. She nodded.

"Of course you do." He tugged again on her hair, not missing the soft moan that escaped her. "Now touch me, dirty girl. Put your hands on me."

She lifted her hands immediately, as if she'd been waiting for the command all along. One warm palm settled on his abdomen, her touch sending ripples of fire through him. Then she reached for his cock, wrapping her fingers tightly around the base and holding on, drawing him even deeper into her mouth.

"Oh...fuck..." This was more intense than he'd ever imagined. Watching her take him and the movement of her breasts as he thrust, the glitter of the chains. Hearing the slight panting sounds she made, the soft moans. Her hand on his stomach was so soft, her touch gentle.

It was too much.

He closed his eyes, the pleasure drawing into a tight, vicious knot.

Victoria's fingers flexed on his abdomen, her nails digging in, her fingers around his cock squeezing. Her mouth was so hot and she was doing things with her tongue, circling the head of his cock, sucking hungrily on him.

"You dirty fucking girl," Connor whispered, his voice hoarse, letting all the filthy things he'd wanted to say out. All the things he'd been keeping inside since he married her. "You beautiful little slut. I'm going to come and it's all your fault."

He wanted to keep this going, wanted to keep fucking her beautiful mouth for as long as he could, but it had been too long and he was too damn hungry.

The orgasm detonated inside him, a nova starburst burning along every single nerve ending he had. Setting him alight. He groaned aloud, his fingers tightening hard in her hair, his rhythm becoming rough and unfocused, his hips jerking as the pleasure uncoiled like a whip.

His last coherent thought was thank God he had a whole night.

Because he was pretty sure he wasn't going to get able to get enough of this.

Victoria rested her head against the heat of Connor's stomach, her heart thundering, the pulse of desire inside her so insistent it was all she could do not to beg. Her scalp tingled from where he'd pulled her hair and the brush of those damn chains against her exquisitely sensitive nipples was enough to make her scream.

You beautiful slut.

Why did she find that so damn hot? Why did she find him calling her dirty so damn hot? Why was being on her knees, taking instructions and sucking him off so arousing she couldn't speak?

It didn't make sense. And yet there had been a moment when it had. When she'd looked up into his eyes and saw how completely he wanted her. How desperate he was. Like he had been the night before. And it had all become beautifully clear.

She could have walked away from him and his orders. Told him where to stick it. But she hadn't wanted to. She wanted this. Desperation and heat and hunger, and all for her.

She closed her eyes, relishing the thick, salty taste of him in her mouth. She hadn't given a guy a blowjob since the night she'd first discovered sex, when Simon Curtis had wanted her to go down on him. She'd enjoyed it then, finding the whole experience new and exciting, amazed at her own feminine power. Simon had been into it too and she'd thought—stupid girl that she was—that his response had meant love. And maybe it had, at least for a little while. Until she'd told him she was pregnant and then he'd told her he didn't care and didn't want to see her again.

Fingers moved in her hair, more tugging that sent little shockwaves of pleasure right through her.

"Up," Connor said, his voice all sexy and rough. "On your feet."

Reluctantly, she eased back from him and did as she was told, rising up from her knees to stand. He adjusted himself, pulling up his zipper unhurriedly, his gaze open and hungry as it swept over her.

She shivered, her mouth dry, the ache between her thighs intensifying.

God, he was hot. Normally he wore suits and that's what she'd come to expect, but not tonight. He was in a pair of old jeans sitting low on his lean hips and a plain, black T-shirt. The knees of his jeans were worn and his feet were bare. A far cry from the polished prosecutor he was during the day. Had he ever worn casual clothing like this when they were together? He must have and yet she couldn't remember it.

His eyes glinted. "See something you like?"

Oh hell. He knew what she wanted. He knew she was desperate. And that knowledge was exposing. Not concealing her feelings was a difficult habit to break and even now, when there was no hiding them, she felt uncertain. Vulnerable.

In fact she hadn't realized till now how vulnerable he actually made her feel.

"Connor," she began, not really knowing what she wanted to say.

Yet he didn't wait for her to finish. "Into the lounge. If you're good, you might just get what you want."

"But—"

His hands rested on her shoulders, turning her around. And then the warmth of his body was up against her back, fingers moving down to rest lightly on the bare skin of her hips. "It's okay, Victoria." His voice was quiet, his breath warm against her neck, near her ear. "It's okay to want it." Then he gave her a gentle push. "Go on. Walk ahead of me. I want to watch you."

Damn it. Did she really need his reassurance? After she'd had him shaking and at her mercy?

Pulling herself together, she walked forward, the high red sandals that had seemed the obvious choice with the thing she was wearing, clicking on the wooden floorboards.

No, she didn't need it. So, she wanted him. Well, he'd wanted her and had let her see it, hadn't hidden it. She'd gotten that from him and hell, she was going to keep it.

The thought kept her going to the end of the hallway that opened up into a massive open plan lounge and dining room.

She walked in and then stopped, overcome by a wave of familiarity.

She remembered this room, with the long windows facing the garden. They'd spent so much money on buying the house and then getting an interior decorator in to renovate it. She'd wanted white because it was calming and restful, and Connor had agreed because he liked the minimalism of it.

So their lounge was a symphony of white. White carpeted floor, white walls. Thick white curtains drawn over those windows. A long white leather couch and a glass coffee table. White armchairs. White dining table and dining chairs. The only things that weren't white were the sleek, black banks of electronics Connor had insisted on—TV and stereo and some kind of house monitoring thing. Oh yes and the black-and-white art photos on the walls.

She'd once loved this room. Especially the peace of it when she was by herself. When Connor wasn't home and she could sit and work without his disturbing presence.

He brushed past her now, walking soundlessly over to the glass liquor cabinet in one corner. He didn't offer her a drink, pouring himself a tumbler of single malt whisky instead. How odd. She didn't think he drank whisky.

Grabbing the tumbler, he walked over to one of the white armchairs and sat down, long legs outstretched and slightly apart. "Sit down," he said and pointed to the floor directly in front of him.

She wanted to protest, say something about how she wasn't a dog and he didn't need to treat her like one. But he was looking at her like she was something good he wanted to eat and she couldn't find it in herself to protest after all. Instead she walked toward him, watching how his gaze moved and shifted. From her mouth to her breasts, to her hips and then lower, down between her thighs, that restless blue flame in his eyes glowing deeper, darker.

It's okay to want...

She found herself breathing hard as she finally came to a stop in front of him, standing between his spread legs. He looked up at her, his gaze searching. "Tell me what you want, Victoria."

A shock of surprise went through her. "What I want? I thought this was all about what you want?"

"It is. I'm going to get off on hearing you say it." He didn't take his eyes off her as he lifted the tumbler and took a sip of whisky. "Go on. I want to hear."

What did she want?

You know...

Well, of course she knew.

"You," she said, proud of the fact that her voice didn't shake. "I want you."

"But I already know that. Where and how do you want me?"

"Why? Are you going to let me give you an order?"

He didn't say anything for a long moment, studying her. And she found herself studying him in return, as if they were fighters measuring each other up. "I might," he said after a moment. "But not if you're being blatantly disobedient."

Her breath caught, strange pleasure twisting inside her. "Disobedient?"

"I asked you to sit."

"Why do you get off on telling me what to do?"

"Why do you get off on being told what to do?" His eyes gleamed, a slight curve to his mouth.

So damn sexy. Sitting there with his long, lean body stretched out on the chair, black hair still spiked up and damp from the shower he must have just had before she'd gotten here. His jeans were unbuttoned, a thin strip of skin showing between the waistband and his T-shirt. His flat, tanned stomach that had felt so hot beneath her hand as she'd sucked him off. Hard muscle and smooth skin...

She was breathless again, shaky with the need to touch him. It was a good question. Why *did* she get off on him telling her what to do? What did she like so much about him being in control?

So you never have to take the blame for liking it...

The voice was a quiet whisper, sitting insistently in the back of her head. And maybe it was true. Maybe it was why she'd put on all the gold chains and nothing else. Why she'd fallen to her knees in the hallway. And even back up in the bar, with Raphael, she'd done all that in response to the challenge in Connor's eyes. Pushing him to tell her what to do, pushing him to take all the blame from her. So she wouldn't have to be responsible for anything that might happen...

"Sit down," he said, his tone quiet and steely.

And she did, going to her knees before him. He leaned forward and reached out, gripping her chin in his fingers, their faces close, his lips millimeters from hers.

She'd never wanted him to close the distance so badly as she did now. Never wanted a kiss as much as she did in this moment.

"You don't want to be dirty, do you, Victoria?"

Her breath was coming faster. "It's not just me."

"No, but I'm willing to come to terms with it. This week I'm letting myself be as dirty, as filthy as I want to be." He leaned forward slightly, his breath against her mouth, warm and smoky with the whisky. "And I'm giving you permission to be dirty too."

"I…." She swallowed. "I don't need your permission."

"No, but you want it. You want it from someone." An inch farther, their lips nearly touching. "So take it from me."

She was almost dizzy with hunger. And when he brushed his mouth against hers, she couldn't stop the soft sound that escaped, or prevent herself from leaning in, wanting more. But it he didn't deepen the kiss, keeping their lips just touching. "Be dirty, Victoria," he murmured. "And tell me what you want."

"I want you to take your clothes off," she said shakily. "I don't want to be the only one who's naked."

He eased back, his gaze searching hers. And she realized belatedly there were layers to that statement she hadn't meant. At least not consciously.

He didn't say anything for a long moment. Then he abruptly lifted his tumbler and drained it, putting it on the side table next to the armchair. And in a smooth, economical movement, pulled his T-shirt up and over his head, throwing it carelessly onto the floor beside the chair.

Victoria took an uneven breath, unable to take her eyes off him as he pushed his jeans down his hips, taking his boxers with them, the tight, hard muscles of his abdomen flexing as he eased them lower. Sliding them down his muscular thighs, long calves and finally off onto the floor.

He kicked them away then resumed his position in the chair, his legs outstretched, his hands on the arms of the chair, staring at her. Gloriously naked and so damn arrogant with it.

Tanned skin and cut muscle. Narrow hips, broad shoulders. A light sprinkling of crisp, black hair. Lean thighs and between them, the curve of his cock, already hard and ready.

She couldn't help herself, putting her hands on his thighs and sliding up, her hands shaking. His skin was hot and she could feel his muscles tighten under her hands. She leaned forward, breathing fast, her hands moving higher to his hips then up over his chest. She'd never touched him like this before. At first she'd never thought she'd ever want to and then, after she'd caught a glimpse of the tiger hiding behind the man, she'd never thought she'd get to.

And now she was.

Be dirty…

She leaned forward even farther and pressed her mouth to his stomach, licking the salt of his skin and inhaling him. The ocean fresh scent of him had become warmer, spicy with male arousal, the heat of his cock pressing between her breasts as she leaned down.

He didn't say anything, letting her touch him for a moment. Then he moved and she felt his body arch over hers as he bent to retrieve something from the floor, the heat of him surrounding her. It was only a second but she felt her heart go still in her chest, an intense, unfamiliar yearning to be held stealing her breath.

Stupid. Why would she want that? She'd never felt the need before so why she should want it now, she had no idea.

Connor sat back and the yearning vanished along with the warmth of him around her. She ignored the emotion, trying to concentrate on the feel of his skin as she moved her hands over him. And then his fingers knotted in her hair, tugging her up, ignoring her gasp of protest.

"Enough." He held something in his other hand. A silver packet. "Put this on me."

A condom. Oh yes, oh God, yes. She took it from him and ripped it open, her hands shaking only a little. Another thing she'd never done for him before. Always he'd been the one to do it.

She gripped the hard heat of him, rolling the latex down, feeling unpracticed and awkward, yet not enough to stop. He tensed under her fingers and when she looked up at him, his eyes had gone dark, like night creeping over a brilliant blue sky. "Get in my lap, dirty girl."

She sucked in a breath. "Facing you?"

"No, away. I want to fuck you like Raphael did. Only this time, you're going to be screaming with my cock in you, not his."

The words were so brutally erotic she found she was trembling as she stood up, beginning to be afraid of the intensity of her desire. Surely she couldn't be this desperate? Surely it was wrong somehow?

His hands were hard on her hips, forcing her to turn around then pulling her back into his lap. It was a shock to feel the heat of his bare skin against hers. Her own skin felt so sensitized she gasped aloud, trembling as he slid a palm over her stomach, beneath the chains around her. But he didn't give her any time to adjust, his fingers curling under the silky fabric of her panties and pulling them ruthlessly aside. Then she was crying out as he slid one finger deeply into her sex. Her hips jerked, her back arching, pleasure flaring, bright as magnesium burning.

He added another finger, working deeper until she was shaking uncontrollably, a dim part of her appalled at how quickly she was almost at the point of orgasm.

"Connor," she gasped as his fingers twisted, the edge so close she could almost taste it.

His free hand slid up her body, the heat of his palm cupping her breast, his thumb circling one nipple in small, gentle movements. It wasn't enough, only prolonging the agony of pleasure.

"Please…"

But the hand between her legs disappeared. "You're not allowed to come, understand?" His voice, dark and ragged in her ear. "Not until I'm ready for you to do so."

He shifted beneath her and she felt the head of his cock pushing against her entrance. But only so far. She squirmed, her hands reaching down, wanting more. Desperate for it. "Connor, please…"

"No." He took her hands and held them down on the arms of the chair, like Raphael had. "Keep your hands here and don't you dare move them."

She didn't even think about disobeying this time, her nails digging into the fabric as he took his hands away from her, shifting again. Sliding deeper.

"Fuck, you're wet." His mouth brushed against her shoulder, her neck. "I wanted to do this slowly but you're all slippery and hot." His voice deepened. "You've got such a greedy little cunt, Victoria. It doesn't want to wait. It's all ready for me right now."

And then he was sliding all the way into her and her head fell back against his shoulder, her body shaking. She was so close, the orgasm she so desperately wanted just out of her reach. His hand was on her breast, gently pinching her nipple, while the other was on her hip, pressing her down.

Oh God, she only needed a little more friction, a little more movement and she'd be there. "Now…" she murmured, hardly even aware she was speaking. "Please…Connor…now…"

"No." His hips moved, his cock sliding out of her, then back in, deeper this time. "Not yet. Sexy, dirty little girls like you have to wait their turn." He thrust again, his hand on her breast and hip firm, and she cried out because again it wasn't enough.

She twisted in his lap, searching for more, but his grip only tightened still further. "Keep still. I'm not done yet." He pinched her nipple hard, the pain not detracting from the pleasure in the slightest, only adding bright sparks to the fire already raging inside her.

"You bastard," she groaned as he thrust harder, delivering another pinch at the same time. "You fucking bastard. I can't…"

"I am. And you can." His breath was harsh in her ear as he moved in a rough, desperate rhythm. "Stop that greedy little cunt of yours from coming, Victoria. You're not allowed. Not until I say."

The hand on her hip moved, sliding between her legs, brushing over her clit in that same light, gentle way as he had when she was with Raphael. A caress at odds with his hard, vicious thrusts and the rough pinch on her nipple.

She wailed, her body arching in his arms. Because it was impossible. No matter how much she wanted to hold out, to do what he said, she knew she wasn't going to be able to. Not with him touching her, or with the filthy words he whispered in her ear, the feel of him inside her.

She tried to fight it, tried to hold back, but her body began to gather itself anyway. "No," she whispered. "I can't."

"Do as you're told, you gorgeous little bitch," he said roughly. Then he bit her, his teeth sinking into the incredibly sensitive skin between shoulder and neck.

It was too much. The hard words, the pain of the bite, the intense pleasure of him inside her, the pinch on her breast. Every nerve ending ignited, pleasure overwhelming her.

She screamed, burning like a torch, and then screamed again, her body bucking against his hold. His voice was in her ear but she didn't hear. There was roaring in her head and lights behind her eyes. And she was lost.

Utterly lost.

And it felt like it took eons to come back to herself, and when she did she was still trembling like a leaf. Connor's hands were on her, stroking down her shoulders and her arms, murmuring in her ear, soothing her. But she didn't feel soothed. She felt stripped bare, oversensitive to every touch and the gentleness of his hands only seemed to make it worse.

"Stop." The word came out harsh but she didn't try to make it sound any less so. "Connor, stop."

The movement of his hands stilled. "What is it?" His voice sounded almost as cracked as hers, yet that didn't make her feel any better. In fact, it only made things worse.

"I need that five minutes." The safe space he'd promised her.

"Sure, but—"

She didn't wait for the rest, pushing away from him and stumbling on shaky legs toward the doorway, heading for the bathroom situated down the hall a little way.

Shutting the door, she cleaned herself up, trying to avoid looking in the mirror, not wanting to even see herself. Because she was sure she was different now and if she was, she didn't want to know.

She couldn't afford to be different. She couldn't be the woman who liked giving blowjobs in the hallway and got off on being called a sexy little bitch. What she needed was to get home, have a shower and wash away all the evidence. Be the person she'd been for the past five years. The person she knew and was familiar with. Comfortable with.

Shivering, she reached for the door handle and pulled it open.

Connor was standing in the hallway outside, muscular arms folded, straight dark brows lowered. He'd pulled on his jeans and now she felt even more exposed given what she was wearing.

"Are you okay?" His frown deepened. "Did I hurt you?"

"No." She took a deep, silent breath. "Is my five minutes up?"

"Yes."

"In that case I've decided I'm going home."

Connor's frown became a scowl. "What?"

"You said after five minutes if I don't want to continue, I don't have to. So I've decided not to continue." She didn't wait for him to protest, brushing past him and going over to where her trench coat still lay in the middle of the hallway. Picking it up, she put it on, belting it tightly around her waist.

"What the hell, Victoria? I made you dinner. Stay for that at least."

Oh God, had he? She glanced at him, seeing the anger flickering in his eyes.

He'll make you pay for that. And you'll love every second.

Her heartbeat accelerated, desire twisting inside her.

No, she couldn't stay. She'd already gone too far, slipped too much from the person she thought herself to be. She couldn't allow herself to slip any further.

"I'm sorry, Connor." And she turned, making for the front door.

"I won't sign those fucking papers," he said roughly. "You know that."

She paused but didn't turn. "You said a week. I'll be here tomorrow."

Then she went out.

Chapter Seven

Connor stared at the computer screen and realized he'd read the same paragraph of the judgment he'd been researching at least five times and still hadn't taken in any of it. Cursing, he pushed himself away from his desk and stalked to the window of his office. It was raining outside, the city buildings nearby lost in another typical Auckland downpour.

He really should be getting on with the mountain of reading he had to do for this case. The kid the police wanted to prosecute had shot his father, but the defense was trying to get the murder charges dropped, claiming the kid had been abused. There had been no concrete evidence of the abuse, but it was clear the kid had hated his father.

Sound familiar?

Connor deliberately didn't think about that. He watched the rain instead.

In all honesty though, it was hard to concentrate on anything with his head so full of the night before. Of Victoria screaming out her orgasm in his arms. Right before she walked out the door without any explanation at all.

Familiar anger simmered inside him, thick and hot, disproportionate to what had happened. Especially since he'd got what he wanted, hot sex and a couple of orgasms. No, she hadn't stayed the whole night and yes, that was disappointing. But surely not enough for him to quite so pissed off with her? After all, she'd promised she'd be back tonight.

Yet that reasoning did nothing for the anger sitting acidly in his gut.

The way she'd left made him wonder if he'd done something wrong, something she didn't like. Hurt her in some way.

Why should you care, though? She said you didn't hurt her. What's the problem?

He let out a breath, staring at the gray rain outside. Christ, he didn't know. He kept thinking of that look in her eyes as she'd knelt at his feet, the one that looked right through him. And then the way she'd touched him in the lounge after he'd taken his clothes off, her hands shaking with desperation. As if she'd been waiting for that moment for a long, long time...

I don't want to be the only one who's naked.

There had been uncertainty in her eyes, fear and reluctance. She'd been conflicted, that much had been clear to him. And no wonder. The sexual intensity between them had been unexpected and difficult to deal with after years of not having it at all.

But perhaps there was more to it than just unexpected chemistry.

Perhaps there was always more to it and you just didn't notice?

Connor scowled at the rain. Christ, why was he thinking about this? It was only sex between them and that's all he wanted. One week, no more. She'd promised him she'd be there tonight so what was the big deal?

One thing he did want was a whole damn night though, not her walking out without explanation again. Which meant if he didn't want a repeat of what happened the night before, he had to figure out exactly what her problem was.

He took his phone out of his pocket, deciding to give her a heads up about what he expected from her tonight in a quick text: *Be prepared tonight to explain why you left the night before.* Then he put it away and sat back down at his desk, trying to get his head back into the case. If he wanted to keep his reputation as a crusader for justice, this murder charge needed to stick.

Five minutes later his phone buzzed. Not a text. A call. He pulled it out and glanced down at the screen. It was Victoria. He pressed the answer button. "If you're calling to tell me you're not coming tonight, please remember our agreement."

There was a small hesitation. "I'm not calling to tell you that."

"Then why? You have a problem with explaining why you ran away?"

"I did not run away."

"Yes, you did. I want to know why."

"You don't get to ask me questions, Connor. That's not what this week is about."

"This week concerns what I want, and if I want an explanation as to why you ran out on me, I will fucking have one."

She was silent, the phone line seeming to vibrate with the anger in his voice. Christ, what the hell was he doing? Letting that anger leak out all over the place. He had to get himself under control. Anger was not good for anyone, him least of all.

Yet he didn't want to take it back. Because for some reason it felt good to let it out, even if it was only a little bit.

"Why do you need an explanation?" she asked finally. "What difference does it make to you why I left?"

Good question.

He dismissed the thought. "Because I want a night, Victoria. A whole night. Which means you need to tell me what went wrong so I can fix it. So it doesn't happen again."

"What if I left because of you? Because you wouldn't sign those damn papers? What if fixing it would only require a signature?"

He sat back in his chair, staring at his computer screen. "Don't tell me you don't want this, Victoria. Don't tell me you aren't looking forward to another night together as much as I am."

She was silent.

"It's not about the signature," he went on when she didn't speak. "It's about the sex, isn't it? And before you say anything, if you tell me you didn't want it and you lied to me last night, then God help me you will *never* get those fucking papers."

The silence stretched out for so long he thought for a second she'd gone. Then she said, "Why do you keep holding that over my head?"

His jaw tightened. "I have to use something. I'd never get anything out of you if I didn't have some kind of leverage."

"You've never wanted anything from me before."

A memory abruptly filtered through the anger inside him. Of coming home that day and finding the letter from Jessica, a child he never knew she had. A child she'd had years ago and hadn't told him. And of the way she'd closed up when he'd forgotten himself and demanded answers, turning her back on him and walking away.

"I have," he said flatly. "I wanted you to tell me about Jessica."

Another long silence, this time crushed by the oppressive weight of the past.

"I'm not the only one with skeletons in their past, Connor," Victoria said quietly.

And he went still, cold seeping through him. No, she couldn't know. He'd buried that past and made sure it stayed buried. No one knew about Damian Blake's little meth empire, or the son he'd tried to drag into business with him. The wife who'd been so badly hurt after he'd thrown her through a window then denied hospital treatment, that it had taken her months to recover. And no one knew the real story about his death the same night, when he was found with a cracked skull on the sidewalk outside his shitty state house. Killed by a disappointed client was the verdict.

But that wasn't the real story. And only Connor knew that.

"I assume you're talking about me?" His voice had gone weirdly flat.

"I'm talking about the fact neither of us have ever been straight with each other. No, I didn't tell you about Jessica, but you're not exactly open about your past either. You have secrets, don't tell me you don't. That tattoo on your back for a start."

The tattoo he'd gotten at eighteen as a reminder. The one he carefully never managed to think about. A sword with the blade following down his spine.

Those who live by the sword shall die by the sword…

"The past has nothing to do with this, Victoria," he said a harsh edge creeping into his tone. "This is about the present. About tonight. If you don't want to tell me why you ran out then don't. But don't expect me to let it go if you do it again. Especially if it concerns me."

She let out a breath. "Okay, you want to know the reason? I found it too much. You, me…what happened."

"'What happened'. Tell it like it is, Victoria."

"Fine. The sex. You, me and the sex. After five years of nothing and then…that. It was just too much."

He scowled at the computer screen in front of him, his jaw tight. "What do you mean too much? I thought you liked it. I thought—"

"I did like it. I liked everything about it. What you did. How you touched me. God, I even liked the way you called me a slut and a bitch." She gave a strange, mirthless laugh. "And that's why it was too much. Because that's not me, Connor. I'm not a bitch. Or a slut. I don't have sex with strangers while my ex-husband watches. And I don't have a week of no-holds barred sex with said ex-husband either. I'm a very successful technology lawyer who is going to London in a few weeks to take up a very prestigious position, not…not…." She trailed off, as if she couldn't bear to say it again.

He hadn't been expecting honesty from her, still less, honesty that involved her actually acknowledging her desires.

He shifted in his chair, uncomfortable. Because he'd never done anything like that either. Never called a woman a slut. Or a bitch. Never told her to keep her wrists down while he fucked her, telling her she couldn't come. It had just come pouring out of him and he hadn't held it back. "There's nothing wrong with liking any of that," he said, a little roughly. "And it has nothing to do with you being a successful lawyer."

"I can't be both, Connor. I just can't."

"You don't have to. At the end of this week, it'll be over anyway so why not let yourself enjoy it while it lasts? That's why I'm doing it."

There was another long silence.

"Why has this never happened between us?" Her voice was quiet. "Why didn't we do this before?"

This was edging into dangerous territory but he had to give her answer. She'd given him one after all. "You never gave me any sign you wanted me to."

"And what would you have done if I had?"

You would have run.

"But you didn't."

"Connor."

He shut his eyes. "I would have told you it couldn't happen."

There was a shocked pause. "But why? And what makes it different now?"

Oh Christ. Did he really have to go into this? Yet he found himself telling her all the same. "Because that's not the kind of marriage I wanted. And it's different now because we only have a week and after that you're leaving."

She was silent, the quiet on the other end of the phone making his chest tighten unexpectedly. Had he hurt her? He probably had.

"Look, I'm—"

"So what kind of marriage did you want?" she demanded abruptly, anger in her tone. "Cold and sexless? Passionless? And now I'm not any of those things, now I'm not your wife, I'm suddenly good enough to fuck?"

"Victoria—"

"We never talked about it, Connor. We never talked about what we wanted from each other. We never talked about anything. Not even whether we loved each other or not."

The words were like stones striking against glass. Sharp and angry. Hard. Each one with the potential to break something, shatter it into pieces. Perhaps shatter him.

No, they'd never talked about love. And with good reason. Because as he knew from experience, love destroyed. It had twisted his father, nearly killed his mother, and he'd be damned if he let it destroy him.

He gripped the phone tight in his hands, the edge digging into his palm. "We had the kind of marriage we both wanted. I didn't see you arguing."

"No." There was bitterness now in her tone. "You're right. I didn't."

At that point there was a knock on his office door then it opened, his PA putting her head around it. "Your one fifteen is here. Do you want me to get them to wait?"

Connor shook his head and held up a hand in a five-minutes sign. "I have to go," he said to Victoria, knowing this was the easy way out and not caring. He really didn't want to keep talking about a marriage that was already over. It didn't help anything. "Be there tonight, seven sharp."

"Any requests as to clothing?" She sounded resigned.

"Tight should do it," he said tersely. "I'll see you then." And ended the call.

Victoria stood before the white paneled front door of their—no, correction, Connor's—house and smoothed down the tight black skirt she wore. She'd worked late that day and had decided not to bother going home, coming straight to Connor's instead.

He'd told her to wear something tight, but her skirt was the only thing about her outfit that was and she wasn't going to make a special trip home just for him. He'd have to put up with her plain dark blue blouse and her black business heels. She wasn't in the mood to make consolations for him, especially not after that phone call.

She couldn't understand why she'd said all those things to him. Asked him all those questions. Like it mattered. Because of course it didn't matter. Their marriage was over and had been for years, and there was no point rehashing things.

We had the kind of marriage we both wanted.

And that was true. Their marriage *had* been exactly what both of them had wanted. Intellectual. Passionless. And completely safe. So why she felt a deep pain in her chest whenever she thought about it was anyone's guess.

But it had nothing to do with them sleeping together. The sex now wouldn't change the past and because it was only for a week, it had no impact on the future either.

In fact, she'd been thinking about it all afternoon and had come to the conclusion he was right. That she shouldn't worry about the intensity of the chemistry burning between them. That it made no difference. After the week was over, it wouldn't matter because she'd be gone, in which case why not indulge? Why not take this as far as it would go? What did she have to lose?

She could put it behind her once the week was up, once she was on her way to London and a new life. Chalk the marriage up to experience and move on. And in the meantime...

In the meantime you can have him in every way you can possibly imagine.

A shiver went through her as she knocked on the door. This time she couldn't tell herself a part of her hadn't been looking forward to tonight, no matter what had happened the night before. That a part of her had been hungry for it since she'd woken up this morning.

She wanted this and he was right. She needed to enjoy it while it lasted.

The door pulled open with a jerk and Connor was standing there in the doorway. He was still in a dark blue suit, white shirt, no tie. His hair looked mussed, his jaw hard and in his eyes the familiar spark of anger. It leapt as he took her in, his gaze dropping to her skirt then back up again.

She arched a brow. "Tight enough for you?"

"It'll do." He stood aside. "Come in."

A strange awkwardness descended as she stepped into the hallway and he shut the door behind her. She didn't quite know what to do with her hands or with the briefcase she was holding.

"Go into the lounge," Connor said.

She did so, aware of his presence behind her as she walked down the hallway and into the white, featureless lounge. She'd never been so conscious of another person in all her life. Of his heat. The fresh scent of his aftershave. The sound of his footsteps on the wooden floor.

His hand brushed hers where she held her briefcase as he took it from her and she nearly jumped at the contact. Trying to calm her racing heart, she turned. "I can do that myself."

"I've got it." He was already taking the briefcase and putting it down on the glass coffee table, where she always used to put it when she came home from work.

She could still feel the brush of his fingers against her skin. The heat lingered like a burn. "So," she began, her voice unsteady despite her best efforts. "Where do you want me?"

He straightened, his gaze like a laser sweeping over her. It made her dry mouthed with want. "Go and sit in that armchair."

"What? Chair sex again? Can't we have something different this time?" She'd meant it to sound ironic, a way to ease her unexpected awkwardness, but it only came out sounding like a stupid attempt at humor.

Connor said nothing, staring at her. Then he came toward her and for some insane reason, she felt like running again. "What's wrong?" he asked abruptly.

She wasn't expecting the question and it took her off guard. Enough that her usual *nothing's wrong* reflex didn't kick in. "I... I'm just tired. I've been handing over my clients to other people and it's been...difficult." Not so much for the clients as for herself. She liked her job and even though she was going somewhere better, leaving it was going to be tough.

A slight crease appeared between Connor's dark brows, the intensity in his eyes wavering. "Leaving is always hard."

There were so many layers in those words. So many meanings whether he'd meant them or not. Either way, she couldn't face them or the type of conversation that would involve.

"So..." She turned toward the armchair. "You want me to sit here?"

Without waiting for a reply, Victoria went over to the armchair they'd made love in the night before and sat, smoothing down her skirt in a habitual motion.

He watched her a moment more, the expression on his face typically unreadable. Then he moved over to where she sat, standing in front of the chair looking down at her. "I don't want you to do anything," he said after a second. "It's my turn to do some...exploration."

Her breathing had sped up at the sound of his slight pause. Exploration sounded...

Good. It sounds pretty damn good.

The palms of her hands were damp. She put them on the arms of the chair, resisting the urge to wipe them on her skirt. "Well, don't let me hold you up. I'm expecting dinner at some point."

Connor's gaze drifted down, stopping at her hips, her lap. "Oh you'll get dinner. But this time I'm getting to eat first."

If his words hadn't been clear, the look in his eyes certainly was.

Victoria's heartbeat was a steady, pulsing beat in her ears, almost a match for the pulse between her thighs. The strange awkwardness was beginning to fade, yet the emotion taking its place wasn't much better. A snaking thread of fear. And it grew as Connor sank slowly to his knees in front of her. As he took the hem of her skirt in his fingers and began to ease it up.

She lowered her gaze, not wanting him to see the trepidation in her eyes, but he must have sensed it anyway because his hands paused.

Dammit.

"Do you need five minutes?" His voice was deep, the edge of it frayed as if he was already deep in the grip of the desire smoldering between them.

"No."

"Victoria."

"I thought it was all 'When I want. Where I want'." She steeled herself then lifted her head, meeting his gaze. "What happened to that?"

His long, sensual mouth tightened. "Don't think I don't know what you're doing."

"Oh, yes? And what's that?"

"You're distancing yourself." The look in his eyes was uncompromising. "You're trying not to feel anything."

"And how would you know?"

His palms were on her bare thighs, the heat from his touch moving up her legs, spreading out. "What do you think I was trying to do last night when you had your mouth around my cock?"

Her throat closed, remembering that searing instant of connection when she'd looked up at him from her knees on the floor, seeing the desire in his gaze. Naked. Unguarded. The intensity of it.

"It didn't work, Victoria," he went on quietly. "I couldn't do it. So I had to trust you. And now it's your turn to trust me. I told you that you could, remember?"

She wanted to deny it again, pretend she wasn't scared. Revealing any of her feelings to him was so difficult. But what would be the point in hiding? When he knew anyway? The time for denial was past.

Connor's thumbs moved slowly on the sensitive skin of her inner thigh, a gentle caress that was somehow even more devastating than the rough lovemaking the night before had been.

"You've never done this before," she said faintly, as if that made any kind of difference.

"Not to you, no."

"But you have..." She stopped, unable to continue.

"Before I married you, yes." His gaze searched hers, studying her. "Because, in case you were wondering, I haven't been with anyone else since we split up."

The confession was a shock. But not as shocking as her response to it, a wave of complete and intense satisfaction. As if it mattered to her. She swallowed. "Why not?"

"I don't know," he said flatly. "I didn't meet anyone I wanted."

Part of her found that disappointing. As if she was waiting for more. Waiting for the *real* reason.

Because I only wanted you.

No, she couldn't let herself want that. She couldn't even let herself think it. Yet the ghost of her need to hear those words lingered all the same.

"That doesn't have to mean anything," she said, as if saying that would exorcise it.

"No," he said. "It doesn't." Yet his hands didn't stop stroking as they moved slightly higher. And his gaze held hers as if *did* mean something after all.

"Connor," she began, her throat utterly dry.

He didn't answer, only pushing the hem of her skirt right up to her waist in a sharp, decisive movement. Then gripping the lacy edge of her panties, he pulled them down and off her.

A fine tremor moved over her skin, the gentle shake before the major earthquake.

"Beautiful," he murmured, his gaze dropping to watch his fingers as they trailed between her thighs. Her breath hissed then caught as he slid a hand beneath her knee and lifted her leg over the arm of the chair, before doing the same with her other leg, spreading her out, warm and wet and open.

There was no anger in his face now, no wariness. "We missed out," he murmured. "All those years together and we never did this. I never got to taste you."

She didn't want to look at him because the expression in his eyes made that pain twist inside her. Regret. Longing. Loneliness. Hunger. A scalpel so sharp and precise it could slice her open and she'd probably never feel the cut until it was too late.

And then he put his fingers on her, holding open the folds of her sex, bending his head between her thighs.

She could feel his breath on her skin, a warm caress all by itself, and she had to shut her eyes because she didn't want to see the inky black of his hair between her legs, or his long, tanned fingers on the vulnerable flesh of her inner thighs. Because it was intimate in a way none of their other encounters had been. Too intimate.

This was an unselfish act. One for her pleasure. And that felt…too much.

She bit her lip hard to stop from crying out when his mouth covered her, the shock of sensation like being plugged into a light socket, and tried to hold out against the wicked pleasure as his tongue slowly licked in long, deep strokes.

But it was like holding back a tidal wave.

The metallic tang of blood filled her mouth, her thighs trembling. His hands slid beneath her buttocks, cupping her like she was a bowl he was drinking from, a guttural sound of approval escaping him. And then his tongue pushed into her, a long, deep slide. Breaking her open.

A moan burst from her, the linen of the armchair giving slightly under the press of her nails as she gripped the arms. Her back arched.

"Yes," he whispered roughly against her. "I want to hear that again, dirty girl. Moan for me, scream for me. Let me know how it feels to have my tongue in that hungry little cunt of yours."

She shuddered as the words worked their magic, undermining her control, her determination to not give in. Oh God, he was going to expose her again. Strip her back to her essence. And leave her with nothing and nowhere to hide.

Was this how he'd felt last night when she'd sucked him off? This naked? This raw?

Helplessly, her eyes opened and she looked down.

And met the deep indigo of his gaze staring back.

A bubble of air stuck in her throat at the expression on his face. At the understanding there.

If there had been any doubt he'd felt the way same last night, it was gone. He had. And he knew exactly what she was feeling now.

His hands moved, as his thumb began a slow, maddening circle around her clit. While he watched her with a hungry, focused look as if he was cataloguing every tiny alteration in her expression.

She couldn't look away. Even when he bent his head, his tongue once again beginning a slow, thorough exploration of her sex. And she kept on looking as his thumb continued to make that maddening movement, his tongue pushing deep inside her.

The sight of his thumb on her, of his mouth against her skin was the most erotic thing she'd ever seen.

Pleasure grew sharp thorns, digging into her. Making her shake. She couldn't keep still, shifting her hips beneath his mouth and the push of his tongue, desperate for the release he seemed hell bent on withholding. Her fingers found the black softness of his hair and she held on tight, short, hard gasps escaping her.

It was too much. She couldn't deal with it. And even though it was suspiciously like begging, she forced it out anyway. "C-Connor. Please…I…now…"

He must have understood because he did something with his tongue and suddenly the bright star of pleasure gathering inside her exploded. And as the shockwave hit, locking her muscles and tearing a hoarse cry from her throat, the blue of his eyes was all she saw. And for the first time, she let herself drown in them.

He kept his cheek pressed to the softness of her inner thigh, the scent and taste of her filling him. Soft heat and musk and salt. A delicate, feminine flavor he knew would haunt his dreams for probably the rest of his life. As would the sight of her watching him as he ate her out. Wide black eyes. Flushed olive skin. Full red lips. The sounds of her ragged breathing. Her husky cries.

She was delicious. He wanted to keep doing this all night. Especially if it meant her falling apart so beautifully for him, the way she'd done just now. It was a rush. A heady power trip. And it felt so good to know he had the same effect on her when he had his mouth on her as she'd had on him the night before.

It was true that oral sex hadn't been what he'd been planning initially. But when she'd come in the door, she'd looked tired. Drawn. And her admission of the fact leaving was going to be difficult felt like she'd given him something, a little piece of herself he hadn't had before.

For the past two nights this had been about him. And as long as she'd gotten off too, he hadn't much cared how selfish that was of him. But when she'd come in this evening, he'd found he did care. That he wanted to give her something, make up for the difficult phone conversation they'd had earlier that day.

Oh, he wasn't entirely altruistic. It wasn't as if he'd never thought about what she would taste like. Plus that power trip…yes, he'd liked that too. And he did have certain plans for this evening involving her relieving the raging hard-on that had his cock pushing against the zipper of his trousers.

But he'd found that fantasies and power trips weren't enough. He'd wanted more. He wanted her to trust him the way he'd trusted her the night before. To know she could fall apart and it would be okay. That she didn't need to leave. That he would keep her safe.

He really didn't know quite why that was important to him, maybe just to give back what she'd given him, but it was important nonetheless.

The glaze of orgasm faded had from her eyes, her breathing slowing.

He rose up on his knees and gently lifted her legs from the arms of the chair, lowering them back down onto the seat. She made no move to help or even to cover herself up, her gaze locked on his face.

"Why did you do that?" she asked in a cracked voice.

"Why did I do what?"

"The…oral sex."

"Because I thought you deserved something for yourself."

Jackie Ashenden

"Oh."

He hesitated then added, "And because I've always wanted to know what you taste like."

There was an expression in her eyes, he couldn't name. "But you never have."

"No." He reached down for her panties he'd discarded on the floor.

"Why not?"

The question hit him unexpectedly hard, in the same way her questions about their marriage had earlier in the day had. Because there were traps there. Snares that would catch him if he wasn't careful.

Slowly he reached up and began to smooth her skirt down, using the movement to gather his thoughts. She didn't stop him, but he could feel her watching him.

I couldn't touch you because I'm afraid of my desire for you. Because control is the only thing that stops me from being an animal like my father.

"Because you didn't seem to want it," he said aloud.

"And yet you never asked."

He sat back on his heels, looking up at her. The flush was still staining her cheeks, her hair half coming out of the bun it had been in when she'd first walked in the door. She looked like a woman thoroughly sated, thoroughly pleasured. Goddamn beautiful. And he wanted her under him, not yet more discussion about a marriage that had never worked in the first place.

"We've already had this discussion, Victoria. Our marriage is over and done with. There's no point going over old ground."

"When you're with me like this, it's like you're a different man," she said as if he hadn't spoken, her dark eyes searching his face. "Why is that, Connor? Why are you trying to hide?"

This time her question was a bullet, precisely aimed and only narrowly missing its target.

Too close. Much, much too close.

She sat forward all of a sudden, the intensity of her gaze like a searchlight. "What are you so afraid of?"

A cold thread of shock ran through him. How the hell had she been able to see that? How did she know?

He stood up in an abrupt, jerky movement. "We're not here to talk. We're here to fuck. That's all. So get up stairs and get your ass in my bed."

She stared at him and he experienced a second's doubt. That she'd actually leave. She'd get up and walk away, and he'd be left standing there all night with a hard-on and the taste of her in his mouth.

But she didn't. Instead she got up out of the chair in a graceful motion. And there was something confronting in her eyes as she slowly peeled down her skirt and kicked it off. Undid the buttons of her blouse and shrugged it down her arms to let it fall on the floor, where her bra joined it seconds later. Then, wearing only her business-like heels, she walked past him.

He clenched his fists wanting to grab her, punish her for daring to challenge him like this. Because he had no doubt it was a challenge. But he managed to keep himself under control enough to turn and watch her as she walked, hips swinging, to the doorway.

Where she paused.

"You can fuck me," she said. "But I'm not staying the night. So if you want me, you're going to have to come now." Another small pause. "And I do mean that literally."

Then she turned and walked out of the room.

Chapter Eight

Victoria was as good as her word. She didn't stay, dressing silently and quickly, leaving without a word not long after one a.m.

He tried to get some sleep after that, but sleep was difficult when he still had the taste of her in his mouth, the smell of her in his nostrils and the memory of her naked body clouding his brain.

Work the next day was a struggle and he was not pleased when Jane, one of his law clerks, stopped him in the reception area as he was finally on his way home. She had a *the shit has just hit the fan* look on her face which instantly made him wary. Because for the first time since he could remember, he didn't want to stay in the office to sort out problems. Victoria was due in a couple of hours and he had a special dinner in mind he wanted to cook her, one he was going to make sure she ate this time.

"What is it?" he asked impatiently, resisting the urge to tell her that whatever it was, he'd deal with it tomorrow.

"Remember Ben's medical records? That the surgery insisted were missing?"

Connor tensed. "Oh Christ. They turned up, didn't they?"

She made a face. "Yep."

Which meant the defense now had incontrovertible proof Ben Andersen had been assaulted by his father. And that was going to make the murder charge next to impossible to stick. Connor would be lucky if he got manslaughter.

Ben Andersen had killed his father, shot him with a rifle, and he was, in all likelihood, going to go free.

Unpunished.

His emotions moved through him like caged beasts, heavy and powerful, pushing at the limits of his control. All so much closer to the surface than they used to be. Rage. Frustration. And there was something else there too, another emotion he kept buried so far down he almost never thought about it. Guilt.

He wanted to throw something, maybe his briefcase, straight through the plate glass of Blake and Associates office windows.

Or maybe what you need is her. Shove her against a wall, take her hard...

Connor let out a silent, measured breath. No. He'd promised himself he wouldn't hold back, but he also wasn't going to take out his emotions on her in that way. He'd done that once before with catastrophic consequences. It wouldn't happen again.

He had to be calm. He had to be in control of himself at all times. And tonight he wouldn't do any of the things he'd planned until after they'd had a civilized dinner. Hell, perhaps they'd even talk before they got down to business. Yes, he'd said talking wasn't the point of their arrangement, but he'd meant the heavy, loaded conversations they'd been having over the past couple of nights. What they needed to stick to were more intellectual and dispassionate topics. Discuss things the way they used to.

Regardless, he needed to prove he was in control of himself before he took control of her, that was for certain. Especially when he felt like this.

"Thank you, Jane," he said calmly, pleased his voice sounded even. "Looks like we're going to have to rethink our strategy."

Jane nodded, oblivious to the storm raging inside him. Waiting for him to issue some kind of command as to what to do.

Which is what he should be doing. Taking control of this situation, dealing with this latest problem in what was proving to be a significantly problematic case. Calling Victoria to cancel tonight…

No.

The denial that rose up inside him was so sure it almost didn't even need thinking about. They only had two more nights and then she would be going. He wouldn't see her again. Christ, he hadn't had enough…

Jane was still waiting, one brow lifted.

"Go home," he said tersely. "Get a good night's sleep. We'll deal with this in the morning."

Both brows lifted. Connor was known for being a slave-driver and being sent home at five was almost unheard of when there was an important case on the line. "Uh… Are you sure?" she asked.

"No. Which means you'd better go now before I change my mind."

She didn't ask twice, disappearing off in the direction of her office to no doubt grab her things and get out of there before he *did* change his mind. Not that he was going to.

Connor turned, striding to the office's entrance and smacking open the double doors, stepping out onto the sidewalk.

It should matter to him that his case was pretty much screwed. That if he wasn't careful Ben Anderson was going to go free and the kid wouldn't end up paying for the crime of taking a life.

And it did matter, of course it did.

But he would deal with that in the morning. Because right now, Victoria mattered more.

Victoria only had to knock once on the door before Connor pulled it open. Clearly he'd been waiting for her to arrive.

He didn't say anything, reaching out and pulling her inside, slamming the door. Then his hands covered her hips and she was being backed up against the wall, the heat of his body pressed to hers. The expression on his face was taut with hunger yet he didn't do anything but stand there, staring down at her. His eyes glittered, his mouth in a tight line.

God, he was so damn sexy. He was all she'd thought about all bloody day. And even the fact she hadn't left his bed 'till after midnight the night before, that it had only been a matter of twelve hours or so since she'd seen him, hadn't dulled the desire.

She wanted him so much. Again.

He leaned his forearms against the wall near her head. Moved in closer, his mouth almost brushing hers. His hips shifted, making her aware he was hard. Yet he didn't kiss her. Didn't make any other kind of move.

She tilted her head back. "Connor?"

"I expect you to stay tonight, are we clear?"

Well, why not? It wasn't as if she had anything better to get back to. "Okay."

There was another long silence.

"No," he said slowly, as if to himself. "No. Not yet." Then his arms dropped and he stepped back, turning away.

Surprised, she stared at the tense line of his shoulders and back. "Hey? What's going on?"

He didn't answer, already walking away from her, down the hallway in the direction of the lounge.

Victoria stared after him, her body aching, an inexplicable disappointment sitting inside her. What the hell was that all about? Was this some new way of tormenting her?

She followed him down the hall and into the lounge. This time the curtains were open, the early spring twilight falling over the neatly manicured garden outside. The garden Connor had insisted on planting himself, an Italian villa style with terraces and pots, boxed hedges and cypresses. A tidy, very controlled kind of garden.

He'd gone over to the doorway to the kitchen area and had paused, turning to glance at her. "Dinner will be ready shortly," he said, curt. "Why don't you sit down and have a drink?"

She ignored his attempt at niceties. "Ah, so are we going to have a discussion now? Because I thought we were just here to 'fuck'."

Connor was silent, a muscle ticking his jaw. Then he said, "I'm too angry right now for that. You'll have to give me an hour or so."

His honesty took her by surprise since she hadn't been expecting to get much of a response. "What are you angry about?"

"A setback at work. It's nothing." His voice was flat, guarded. A familiar tone. The one he always used when she was intruding. The one that told her not to ask any more questions.

Fuck that.

A shot of something hot and angry pierced her. He couldn't tell her he was "too angry" only to fob her off with crap like "setbacks at work". Not when he'd been insisting on certain truths from her. It didn't work that way.

"Oh well," she said coolly. "In that case, you won't mind if I don't stay for dinner. I have some work to do at home so—"

"What the hell are you talking about?" Anger glittered in his gaze. "You can't leave. We've only got two more nights left."

"Then if you want them, you're going to have to give me more than damn 'setbacks', Connor. Especially when you keep demanding the truth from me."

His mouth hardened. "I don't have to give you a thing."

"No. And neither do I." She didn't wait for him to reply, turning and marching back toward the doorway.

Only to get halfway across the room and come to a halt as his long, warm fingers wrapped around her upper arm.

"Don't push me, Victoria," he growled softly, pulling her against him.

Her heart was thumping, adrenaline firing in her blood, excitement gathering inside her. Because she had power here too and she couldn't let herself forget it. He might be able to get things out of her, but she could get things out of him if she managed it right. She *could* push him. And perhaps it would do both of them good if she did.

"Why shouldn't I push you?" She didn't move, concentrating on the heat of him along her spine and the grip of his hand on her arm. "Maybe that's what you need, Connor. Maybe that's what you really want from me. You want to be pushed."

"And you have no idea what you're talking about. You don't want me when I'm like this, you really don't."

They'd never tested each other. Had always accepted each other's boundaries. Yet there was something exhilarating about taunting him like this. Like poking a sleeping tiger with a stick to see what would happen, half of her terrified of waking it up, the other half desperate to see it roused, wanting the excitement of the danger.

"Interesting how you have no problem telling me what I want. But when I tell you the same thing, it's all 'you have no idea'." She put a hand behind her, gripped the hard muscle of his thigh. "What are you afraid of? Should I be worried you're going to be the one running out tonight?"

His hold tightened, pulling her more firmly against his body. "I will not be running away."

"Oh no? Then why did you in the hallway? You were going to take me, weren't you? You were going to push me up against that wall and fuck me. But you didn't. Why not? You don't think I can take it? Is that what you're worried about?"

His mouth was by her ear, rough and hot. "Stop talking, Victoria."

But she couldn't seem to shut herself up. Her heart was racing and she knew she was playing with fire and yet it felt good to test those boundaries for a change. Push those limits. Change things.

"Perhaps I want you angry, Connor Blake," she murmured thickly. "Perhaps I prefer you angry. Because it's a damn sight more exciting than you acting like you have a permanent stick up your—"

But she didn't get to finish. With a hard jerk, Connor pulled her around.

And then his mouth was on hers, demanding and hot as fire, and she was being propelled back fast. The wall hit her back, Connor pressed hard to her front, six foot four of long, lean muscle, crushing her. On the shelf next to her, a fragile white vase teetered and fell onto the floor, knocked off by the impact and even though it fell on carpet, it broke.

Victoria barely noticed. Connor didn't give her room and he didn't let up, his mouth on hers devouring her like she was his last meal.

It was glorious.

She raised her hands to his shirt and gripped the cotton, tearing it apart so she could get her hands on his body, touch his bare skin. He cursed against her mouth. "Fuck. Did I say you could touch me?"

Victoria spread her hands out on the hot, smooth skin of his chest. "Did I say you could kiss me, prick?"

For an answer he crushed her mouth under his again, his tongue pushing inside, exploring her, demanding more. She gave it to him, panting, taking what she wanted as well. And then she felt his hands at her skirt, jerking it up in a sharp movement, stitches ripping. His fingers curling around the waistband of her panties, tearing them aside, sliding between her thighs and into the slick folds of her sex.

She cried out against his lips as a deep, vicious pleasure caught her in its grip.

He grabbed her wrists in his free hand and pushed them up and over her head, pinning them against the wall. Then he curled his fingers inside her, pushing deeper, and she shuddered helplessly.

"Look at me," he ordered roughly. "Keep your eyes on me, dirty little girl."

And she did, the pleasure twisting even tighter at the furious, savage look in his eyes. He was unguarded, an elemental, raw kind of passion radiating from him that stole her breath. That made her want to demand even more from him.

"Why?" she panted. "Afraid of losing your nerve again?"

"Shut your mouth, beautiful." He flexed his fingers inside, wrenching a desperate moan from her.

Oh God, she was trembling with excitement and exhilaration. From the feel of his fingers and the press of his body, the musky scent of aroused male. The hard, blazing glitter of his eyes. And it hit her with the force of a blow that she wouldn't go back to what they'd had before, even if Jessica's letter hadn't arrived. Even if they were still together.

She didn't want that passionless, cold existence. She wanted *this*. She craved it. And she wanted it from him.

"No," she said, breathless. "I will not shut my mouth."

He bared his teeth. "Then you're asking for fucking trouble."

"Yes, that's exactly what I'm asking for." She leaned forward just the tiniest bit, inches away from the storm in his eyes. "I want it, Connor. I want you angry. I want you raging. I want you wild. So do it. Give it to me."

His gaze darkened and she could see the pulse at the base of his throat beating fast. But he was holding back. Like he was standing right in front of a line he didn't want to cross.

So she crossed it for him.

She kissed him, sinking her teeth into his lower lip. Biting him hard.

He made a growling sound in his throat and jerked his head away, his chest heaving. Then he pulled his fingers out of her and released her wrists, putting his hands on her hips and turning her so she was facing the wall. Shoving her up against it.

She turned her head, the cool paint pressing against her cheek, trying to get a breath because she was so turned on, so excited she could barely breathe. His hand settled on the back of her neck in a heavy, possessive hold, keeping her exactly where she was. Then she felt him rip away the rest of her panties so she was bare from the waist down.

"Keep still," he breathed in her ear. "Don't fucking move."

But she wanted to move. She wanted to keep pushing. So she began to turn around. He cursed and shoved her back against the wall, and this time he took her hands and pinned them above her head again. Victoria pulled against him, the movement prompting another of the knickknacks in the shelves nearby to fall. And perversely it gave her pleasure to see it break.

In fact, she wouldn't mind if everything in this pristine, sterile fucking room broke. If the couches were ripped, stuffing strewn everywhere. The electronics pulled from the wall and smashed on the floor. The stupid black-and-white art pictures thrown over chairs, the canvases ripped.

Because she didn't want white and pristine and sterile. She didn't want calm. Not anymore.

Connor growled again as she pulled against his hold, plastering her to the wall with his body. "Beautiful little bitch." His breath was against her neck. "You want me to fuck you hard? Be my filthy slut?"

She struggled to get a breath, her heartbeat so loud it was like a plane taking off. "You can try. But I'm not sure you're man enough for me."

He laughed, a low, savage sound that wound her excitement even tighter. "You think you can play with me, don't you, dirty girl? Well, we'll see who's in charge when I'm buried balls deep in your cunt." His fingers tightened around her wrists. "Legs apart. Now."

The dirty talk was insanely hot, his hard grip even hotter. "Make me."

He obliged, kicking her legs apart. "That was easy. But then you don't really want to make this difficult for me, do you? Not when you're so fucking greedy for me."

She was shivering now, feeling sharp movements behind her. Then came the rip of foil and he must have torn the condom packet open with his teeth because his grip on her wrists didn't falter. She couldn't help herself, shoving back against him, thrilled when he cursed viciously and shoved back, her cheek pressed hard to the wall.

And then his cock was pushing inside her in a deep, hard thrust.

"Oh...God...." The words were sharp, desperate. "Connor..."

He didn't pause and he didn't hold back, driving into her, each thrust shoving her against the wall. "You want more and harder, you have to tell me. Give me the words, Victoria." His hips flexed, his voice rougher, darker. "And you'd better make it fucking dirty otherwise you won't get what you want."

She closed her eyes, feeling the slide of his cock, the stretch of her sex around him, the weight of his body pinning her. She was surrounded by heat and power, the sheer force of his fury. It was like being in the middle of a hurricane and she loved every second.

"Fuck me," she whispered. "Fuck me harder."

"Where shall I fuck you, Victoria? Where do you want my cock?"

"I want it in...my pussy."

He reached her with his free hand, jerking on her blouse and pulling it open. "I said make it dirty."

She didn't like to swear and she most especially didn't like the word he wanted from her. But it was so erotic hearing him say it to her and she wanted to give it back. Especially when his hand roughly pushed her bra up and took her breast in his palm. "I want..." He squeezed her, pinched her nipple. "I want your cock in my c-cunt."

"Louder." He thrust again. "I didn't hear you."

She lost patience. "Shut up and fuck me, you prick!" She shoved back against him again. "Harder. I want it harder!"

And he did. Hard and deep, and with each thrust she was sure she could feel the walls tremble. Or maybe that was just her. Maybe that was just the orgasm beginning to build like lava underneath a volcano. Heavy and hot and unstoppable.

More things fell off the shelf but neither of them noticed.

There was nothing but panting and sweat and raw, animal lust.

He drove himself inside her and she could feel herself begin to break apart, cracking like the vase. Cool and calm Victoria Blake, shattering. Leaving someone else in her place.

Connor's dirty girl.

Then the hand on her breast dropped between her legs, pinching her clit, and she came fast and she came hard, sobbing against the wall as he found his own release, his hoarse cry loud in her ear.

For a long time she didn't move and neither did he, his breathing fast and hot against her neck. He'd let go of her wrists and it was only his arm sliding around her waist that kept her upright.

The high of the orgasm began to fade, leaving her feeling raw and bruised and strangely frightened for reasons she didn't understand.

Then his mouth moved against her neck, a soft brush of his lips so at odds with the roughness of the sex they'd just had, that she didn't know quite what to do. A shiver wracked her. It was gentle, almost...tender.

"Don't run away, Victoria," he whispered. "Stay the night. Please."

Chapter Nine

He shouldn't have said it like that, as if he was helpless and needy when he wasn't either of those things. And yet he couldn't stop the words from coming out.

She smelled of passion and sex. Rain-drowned magnolia and musk. Her softness against him was like a gift he didn't know he'd wanted.

Christ, he thought he'd been so good, forcing himself not to take her in the hallway. Forcing himself to keep control and walk away. But she hadn't let him. She'd made him confront her, take her. Give her his anger and now he felt…hollowed out.

He wanted to get away from her, get some space to put himself back together again and yet he didn't want to let her go. It was as if the smell of her, the feel of her, filled the empty, hollowed out space in a way he didn't understand and yet craved anyway.

Victoria was silent, standing motionless in front of him.

And he wished he'd never phrased it like a fucking question. Wished he'd just ordered her upstairs and into his bed like he had the night before because then she'd have to do it.

"I'm not running," she said at last, her voice frayed as torn silk. "You were clear what you wanted."

He didn't know why he felt such relief but he did all the same. And he didn't want to step away from her, wanted to keep holding her like this, her body against his, savoring the unfamiliar joys of physical closeness while he could.

Eventually though, he knew he had to move. Slowly, he withdrew from her then smoothed down her skirt, noticing the fabric had torn. Jesus Christ. "I'm sorry. I'm going to have to buy you a new skirt."

"It's okay. I don't like skirts much anyway." She was leaning against the wall as if she couldn't move, her forehead pressed to the smooth expanse of paint. Her hair, which had been in her usual neat work bun, had come loose, inky black curls falling down over her neck and shoulders.

He reached up and began to gently tuck the silky strands back into the bun. Still she didn't move, allowing him to tidy her hair without comment. As he neatened up the last lock, he noticed marks on the side of her neck. The marks of his teeth.

A small current of ice wound through him.

Blood everywhere. His mother lying unconscious amidst the shattered glass. His father standing there, still shouting at her. So much violence. That's all his father was about. Live by the sword, die by the sword...

And you're just the same.

He pushed away from her, his hands shaking. "Why don't you go upstairs and have a shower? I'll get dinner ready."

Victoria turned around and leaned back against the wall. Her eyes were half-closed, her mouth red and kiss-swollen. And he could feel the hunger for her rise in him again. The need to tear off her clothes and have her bare skin against his.

She gave him a sultry, indolent look. "You don't want to join me?"

He did. But he wasn't going to. He needed the time to collect himself and more sex wasn't going to do that. "Not yet." Turning away, he added, "This dinner won't cook itself."

She didn't press so he left her to it, using the bathroom downstairs to clean himself up then going back into the kitchen to see to the food he'd put in the oven earlier.

He'd made a lamb tagine as soon as he'd gotten home from work, remembering a conversation they'd had years before about places she'd always wanted to visit. Morocco and the Middle East had featured highly. So he'd cooked something he hoped she might like, adding a cucumber and tomato salad and couscous. The simple task of cutting up the tomatoes and the cucumber was calming, the wild beat of his heart steadying as he put them into a plain white bowl.

Okay, so he'd promised himself he wouldn't hold back with her. That he'd give in to every dark urge he'd ever had. But he didn't like how those urges overtook him, overpowered him. How they seemed to hook into the anger living just beneath the surface of his skin.

He'd always prided himself on the fact he treated women with respect. That he didn't take part and actively frowned on the casual sexism that so often cropped up in his job. It was another thing that set him apart from his father, who'd treated his wife like she was his own personal slave.

And yet here he was, shoving a woman against a wall. Calling her a bitch. A slut. Tearing her clothing. Biting her. Not just any woman either. The woman who was his wife.

He stared down at the bowl in front of him, at the green and red of the fresh vegetables.

Had this week been a mistake? Was letting himself off the leash dangerous? Both for her and for him? Because God knew, he'd never forgive himself if anything happened to her. If he hurt her. He wasn't a man who hurt women. He'd *never* be that man.

Yet something wasn't right. The setback with the Anderson case was fairly major, but he'd had setbacks with cases before and hadn't felt nearly so furious as he had when he'd gotten home that day. He certainly had never taken out that anger and frustration on anyone else before.

What was happening to him?

Perhaps you should call it off? Sign the papers now?

Well, that was one way to fix it. And yet the thought of it was… not acceptable. He wasn't ready to end the week. Despite the dangers, he wanted more. Which made him not only a selfish prick but a sick one too.

"Hey? Are you okay?"

He looked up from the salad and his heart nearly stopped.

Victoria was leaning against the doorframe, her arms folded. Her hair was loose and damp down her back, and all she wore was one of his white business shirts. The hem came down to mid-thigh, leaving her legs bare and if he wasn't very much mistaken, she wasn't even wearing underwear.

"I'm fine." He straightened, desire igniting inside him once more. "Did I say you could borrow one of my shirts?"

Her mouth curved, as if his response had pleased her. "No. But seeing as how you ruined both my skirt and my panties, you kind of owed me."

Something else had joined the desire slowly hardening his cock and making his blood pump hard. A possessive kind of feeling, one that approved very much of her in his shirt. *Mine*, it said.

"Keep it on," he heard himself say. "You look fucking sexy. And I like seeing you in something of mine."

Her gaze held his for a long moment then her smile deepened, pink glazing the smooth olive of her cheekbones. "Well, thank you. I rather like it myself. Anyway, that smells good."

"Go sit down and I'll bring it out." Best they ate now. Before he grabbed her and had her on one of the kitchen counters.

They ate at the big glass and white wrought iron dining table they'd both chosen when they'd first bought the house. They'd both liked the clean lines and restrained elegance of it, but they almost never sat there eating dinner together. Their schedules had always been too busy.

So it was strange to sit there, eating a meal he'd prepared, watching her sit opposite wearing nothing but one of his business shirts, her only other adornment the black cloud of hair he was rapidly becoming obsessed with.

She wasn't the reserved, cool woman he'd married now. She was someone else, somehow different. And he found himself watching her, fascinated.

"This is good," she said, forking up some lamb. "Middle Eastern, right?"

"It's a lamb tagine. From Morocco. You said you wanted to visit it once."

She raised a brow. "You remembered that?"

Connor leaned back in his chair, idly playing with the glass of red wine he held. "The night we met. At the law school ball. You said you wanted to travel and that you wanted to go to Morocco."

"God, really? That was years ago."

It had been but it was fixed in his memory. She'd worn a plain, classy black dress, different to all the other women in their tight, glittery outfits. He'd been drawn to her cool intellect and the air of reserve about her, admiring both qualities. There had been nothing overly passionate or intense about her and he'd appreciated that. Been attracted to it because it had suited him. He hadn't been looking for either passion or intensity.

"I still remember."

She gave him a look he couldn't interpret, then glanced away, chewing thoughtfully on her lamb before swallowing and reaching for her wine. "Well, perhaps I'll actually get to go while I'm in England. Be nice to travel somewhere different."

He shifted in his chair, trying to tear his gaze from the view of her bare thighs he could see through the glass of the tabletop. She had her legs tucked under her, the hem of the shirt hiding the shadowed space between her thighs. But still he couldn't seem to stop looking.

"What about Jessica?" he asked, distracted.

There was a pause.

"I'm not sure you have the right to ask me that question."

Her tone was cool, even. A return of the Victoria he'd married, not the sexy woman with the sensual smile who had greeted him in the kitchen earlier.

He finally tore his gaze from her legs and met her dark eyes. There was no heat in them now, or that sensual amusement of before. They were cold, a door slamming shut in his face.

It made him angry for some reason. "I don't care whether I have the right or not. Will you let her know you're going?"

Her face had gotten a hard, set look. The one she'd had when he'd confronted her about the letter. The one that had so often been on her face the last couple of years. "No," she said flatly. "I won't."

He should leave it alone, he really should. But he didn't. "Why not? Don't you think she'd want to know?"

Carefully Victoria set her wine glass down. "I don't want to discuss Jessica with you, Connor. So can we change the subject please?"

"Why?"

Her expression didn't change. "I'm asking nicely."

No, he didn't want her looking at him like this. Like he was a stranger or one of her colleagues, or someone she'd only just met.

You were happy enough with it for five years.

Yeah, well, he wasn't happy with it anymore. Not now he knew what it was like when she was wild with passion, when she looked at him with fire in her brown eyes, wanting him. Needing him. He wanted more of *that* not this…cold, shutdown gaze.

"Fuck nicely," he said, deliberately coarse. "We've had *nice* for too damn long, don't you think? Why don't you just answer the question for once in your life?"

And finally, her expression cracked, a hint of furious anger leaking out before she looked away, back down at the table. "Fine. Then you can tell me about that tattoo on your back. The one you've never said a word about."

Fuck, turnabout was a bitch.

Silence fell, oppressive as storm clouds on a mountaintop.

You don't have to tell her everything. You don't have to tell her what a fucking hypocrite you are and always have been.

Connor raised his glass and drained it, the wine sitting warm and heavy inside him. "That tattoo? Okay, it's meant to be a reminder. Live by the sword, die by the sword. I was eighteen when I got it so you'll forgive me if I'm a little embarrassed about it now."

She stared at him, the surprise obvious on her face. "Oh. Why did you need a reminder like that?"

He'd never mentioned his family to her. Not once. And he really didn't want to talk about them now. "Because I grew up in a shitty area, around a lot of violence. And I didn't want to turn into one of the people I grew up with. Does that answer your question?"

Her gaze held his for a second then it flickered away again, the set expression on her face fading. But her mouth still had a tight cast to it. "Yes," she said after a moment. "It does." She paused. "Jessica didn't ask me to contact her. So I've decided to leave it at that." There was no emotion in her voice, only a cool statement of fact.

Connor studied her. He couldn't tell what she was thinking, what she was feeling. Whether this was painful or otherwise for her. But he remembered the way she'd absolutely refused to talk to him about the letter. About Jessica. And how, as she'd walked out of the house, he could have sworn he'd seen the briefest flash of agony in her eyes.

"Why?" he said, pushing, even though he knew it wasn't a good idea. "Don't you want to know about her?"

"No. I think it's best if I don't." Her tone said plainly this was the end of the discussion.

But for some reason he couldn't leave it alone. "Why not? Don't you think your daughter would want to know her mother?"

"That's my decision, Connor."

"Are you afraid to meet her? Is that what the problem is?"

She looked at him, her expression a mask. "It's got nothing to do with you, so how about you stop asking me about it?"

No, he was wrong. He did know what she was feeling. She was in pain, he could see it now. In the way she avoided the subject, in the tightness around her eyes and mouth. And it was so bloody obvious he didn't know why he'd never seen it before.

Because you've never seen her face relaxed in passion, in heat and pleasure before. Now you know the difference.

Again that strange tightening in his chest. Like regret.

He held her gaze. "She wouldn't have sent that letter if she didn't want contact, Victoria."

"Screw you," Victoria said abruptly, anger bleeding into her voice. "What gives you the right to pass comment? You know nothing about either the situation or her, so why don't you shut up?" She shoved away her plate. "You wanted me to stay the night so I'm staying. But I'm not having heart-to-heart chats about our lives, our marriage or anything else. You wanted to fuck me, so fuck me."

Connor's blue-eyed gaze felt like broken glass cutting into her. Slicing deep into sensitive flesh with the precision of a scalpel, excising the truth from her. And she held it because to look away would mean he was right, she was afraid.

But he wasn't right. Jessica didn't want contact. If she had, she'd have said something in the letter and she hadn't. And Victoria was happy with that. It had been enough to know her daughter had had a good life, a successful job, was loved by her adoptive family. Enough to know her decision to give Jessica up for adoption had been the right one. The only one.

She didn't need to know anything more.

But that didn't stop the dull ache that settled in her gut, the heavy familiar feeling of guilt. A guilt she'd spent years and years pretending she didn't feel.

That was the problem with emotions. You let one in and a whole lot more started piling in on top of them. God, she should never have started this with Connor. Never. Admitting to lust, to desire, had been a mistake. Yet now she couldn't get enough. It was all she'd thought about since she'd come downstairs wearing his shirt.

God, if she got him thinking about sex then maybe he'd shut the hell up about Jessica.

But he just looked at her, stared right into her. "I changed my mind. Maybe we're not here just to fuck after all, Victoria. Maybe talking would be a good idea for a change."

"So for five years you were happy to say nothing at all, and *now* you want to talk?" She shoved her chair back and stood up. "Well, I'm sorry it doesn't work that way. This time I do not want to talk. I want to fuck." She said the word with relish as she moved around the table to where he sat, halting beside his chair. "So are you good with that or not?"

He tipped his head back, looking up at her. He'd gotten rid of his ripped shirt and he was just sitting there in his suit pants, all that beautiful bare chest and flexing abs on display.

At least desire was simple. It didn't hurt and it didn't expect things from her. And it sure as hell didn't make her feel guilty.

"You're angry," he said quietly. "Why?"

"Because you completely ignored me when I told you I didn't want to talk about it. Because you keep on pushing." His chair had been moved back a little way, giving her enough room to lift a leg and slide into his lap, straddling him. He didn't say a word as she did so, only watching her, his gaze enigmatic.

"Anyway," she went on, settling herself, the hard edge of the table at her back. "I'm not the only one who's angry. You didn't want to talk about your tattoo either." She shifted her hips, feeling the ridge of his steadily growing erection press against her. "So how about we not talk about any of it, okay?"

He remained still, his attention firmly on her face. "Why don't you want to talk to me, Victoria?" he asked, his voice soft. "Are you afraid of me?"

Something caught painfully inside her. "No, of course I'm not afraid. And why should I talk to you? You're Mr. Perfect, Connor Blake. With your amazing career and your perfect life. What would you know about making mistakes?" She found she was breathing hard, bitterness rising at the back of her throat. Why had she said that to him? Why had she given herself away like that?

The expression on his face changed, shadows moving in his eyes. He sat forward suddenly, their faces inches apart. "Perfect? Is that what you think? Jesus fucking Christ, you don't want to know about the mistakes I've made."

"Oh, sure you have," she said, anger making her voice sharp. "Don't tell me, you didn't return a library book on time? Forgot to pay your power bill once?"

His fingers closed around her upper arms, his grip tight. Something dangerous glittered in his eyes. "Like I said, you don't want to know."

And she felt it, the desire for him. The hunger rising. Responding to that intensity, that fierce, dangerous look. She was naked under the shirt, the wool of his suit pants rough against her skin, pressing against the tender flesh between her thighs. It felt so good. He felt so good. It made her want to be so bad.

She shifted her hips against him, a slow undulation, watching his pupils dilate in response. "Why not? What could you have done that was so very wrong, Connor?"

"I can't tell you. I can't ever tell anyone."

"I had a baby when I was sixteen after I lost my virginity at a school dance. I gave her up because I wanted to make my parents proud of me and they had sacrificed too much already." She undulated again, staring into his face. "What's worse than giving up your own child for your parent's approval?"

He stared at her a long moment. Then abruptly his mouth twisted and his fingers released her. "No, Victoria. Not tonight."

No more.

She leaned forward before she was even aware of doing so, shoving her fingers into the dark silk of his hair, dragging his head back by force. He stiffened, staring up at her as she leaned over him. But he didn't move.

"Tell me," she said quietly, fiercely. "Tell me what your mistake was."

"Your mistake was bringing a life into this world." His lips drew back, his teeth bared, the look in his eyes abruptly savage. "My mistake was taking one out of it."

"What?" she said blankly.

He didn't reply straight away, shaking his head loose of her hands then shoving his chair back farther. Putting his hands on her hips, he gently pushed her off him and stood.

She stared at him as the truth began to penetrate, followed by a wave of slow moving shock.

"I'll leave you to work that one out for yourself," he said, the paused. "You can stay if you like. There are blankets in the hall cupboard. Or you may prefer to leave. I think that's what I'd prefer."

He didn't wait for her to say anything. He only turned and left the room.

She heard him go out into the hallway, his footstep on the stairs. Then the hard click of the bedroom door above. Shutting her out.

Your mistake was bringing a life into this world.

My mistake was taking one out of it.

Holy God.

Chapter Ten

Connor stalked over to the window of his bedroom then stalked over to the bed and back to the window again. He couldn't sit down, couldn't stay still.

He'd told her. Why the fuck had he told her? The thing he'd been hiding all this time. The thing that made him the biggest hypocrite in the history of the world.

Connor Blake, top police prosecutor, respected lawyer.

Murderer.

He'd never told anyone. He'd promised his mother as she was recovering in the hospital that he wouldn't and he hadn't. But it was a secret that had swallowed him whole. Eaten him up from the inside, leaving him just a shell. A perfect, gleaming façade while inside…

Darkness. Taint.

And he'd told because…well, because she'd sat in his lap, wild and beautiful. In his shirt, naked, with her fingers in his hair. Demanding an answer from him in a way she'd never done before. A way no one had ever done.

He'd kept hold of that secret for so long and she'd obviously expected it to be no big deal, whatever it was he was going to tell her. So he'd thrown it at her like a grenade. Wanting it to explode and shatter the thing growing between them. The warmth and the heat and the emptiness inside him that wanted something to fill it.

He couldn't have it. Which meant he couldn't afford to feel it.

Behind him, he heard the door slam open, banging off the wall, and he turned 'round sharply.

Victoria stood there, her black hair curling around her face, her dark eyes full of anger. "What the hell are you doing?" she demanded, her voice rising. "You can't just tell me something like that then leave. I want a fucking explanation!"

The word sounded deliciously filthy in her prim mouth and he cursed himself for noticing. It made him even more aware of what an extremely bad job he was doing of pretending to be a good man. "An explanation? You mean you want to know who I killed? And why? Better that you leave, Victoria. The less you know, the better."

"No." She lifted her chin and came around the big white bed they'd hardly ever shared, preferring to stay in their own separate rooms like an eighteenth century aristocratic couple. "You gave that to me. You told me. And it's up to you to explain."

He watched her come, remaining where he was, standing by the window with his arms folded. "And you were the one who asked for it. I gave you the truth."

"And I gave you mine."

"So you had a baby at sixteen. That must have been hard."

She stopped directly into front of him, staring right at him. "Are we going to play this game? The *I've got a worse secret than you* game? Because if we are, I surrender. Yours is worse than mine. Now tell me what happened."

The truth. The whole truth and nothing but the truth…

He'd already told her the worst. Might as well give her the rest.

"My father was a dealer, part of a meth ring. He was violent, as most of those kinds of men are, and arrogant and thought he owned the world. He certainly thought he owned me and my mother. He used to tell me I needed to harden up if I wanted to take over the business after him. I needed to be strong and all the punches and kicks were part of him making me stronger. Making me a man." Telling her this should have been difficult, should have felt like it was being dragged from him, but it wasn't. It was easy. As if he'd been waiting for the chance to tell her all along. "Christ, like I wanted to be a man like him. Anyway, Dad never used to try his product, but I guess he thought he was above anything as petty as mere addiction because one night he took some. And didn't handle it well. My mother got the brunt of it. He ended up throwing her through a window."

Victoria's eyes widened. But she didn't say anything.

"I remember him standing over her," Connor went on, the words spilling out from him with so much ease it was a wonder he'd managed to keep it secret for so long. "And there was blood everywhere, and he was laughing. Cursing her. I tried to get him to call an ambulance because Mum had so many cuts, but he wouldn't. He wouldn't let me near her either, kept shoving me onto the ground.

"And when I got up the last time, I realized for the first time I was taller than he was. I was behind him, and he wasn't looking. So I hit him and he went down. And it was so *fucking* good to see him on the ground like that. I kept hitting him. I couldn't stop myself. I was just so angry at him. For all the pain he'd doled out over the years, pain he'd caused my mum and myself. Eventually I stopped when I saw he wasn't moving. Then I went and got my mother and took her to hospital." He took a breath. "We got a call the next morning to say Dad had been found on the sidewalk outside our house and he was dead. Fractured skull."

Victoria didn't look away from him and he couldn't read the expression in her eyes.

But he held her gaze, giving her the truth because that's what she'd wanted. "And you know what I felt? I was relieved. I was just so fucking grateful the prick was dead. I killed my own father with my bare hands and all I felt was glad." And if he concentrated, he could feel it still, the remembrance of that relief. No guilt. Just relief. "But of course, you can't kill someone and expect to get away with it. And I didn't expect that. I wanted to go to the police and hand myself in, but my mother wouldn't let me. She was afraid of reprisals from the people Dad was involved with, and I was the only thing she had. She didn't want to lose me. So she made me promise to keep quiet about it and not say a word." He could feel his mouth curve in a mirthless smile. "Turned out I needn't have worried. The police had already pinned it on a disgruntled client and they were less than interested in me."

And still she didn't say anything, that dark gaze of hers looking at him, past the pristine shell of a man, to the raging, violent eighteen-year-old he'd once been.

Christ, she'd have made an excellent judge.

"Turn around," she said and it was an order, pure and simple.

So he did, because why not? He'd given her everything. He had nothing left to hide behind.

"Live by the sword," she murmured.

He felt the lightest touch, her fingers tracing the tattoo on his back. It made the hairs on the back of his neck stand up. He stared at the black window and the evening beyond it. "I got it that night."

"Your penance."

It wasn't a question and he wasn't surprised by her observation. She'd always been sharp. "I had to pay for what I did or at least that's what I thought at the time. I wanted to make sure I never forgot. Or maybe it was only punishment for not caring the bastard was dead and I killed him."

Her hand was suddenly pressed flat against his back, between his shoulder blades, the heat of her palm burning on his skin. "Let's get this straight," she said quietly and with such certainty he felt a part of him go quiet and still. "A beaten, abused young man, trying to save his mother's life is not a murderer. From a purely legal perspective, Connor, you had no intent to kill. It was manslaughter."

He gave a harsh laugh, trying to ignore the feel of her hand because it was a pleasure he sure as hell didn't deserve. "How do you know I didn't have intent? I was glad he died. And I was even glad I was the one who'd taken him out." The night outside pressed in on him, like the darkness inside him pressing against the clean, smooth shell of the man he'd been pretending to be for so long he'd forgotten it wasn't actually him.

Her fault. She makes you remember.

With her hands and her mouth, and the tight, wet heat of her pussy around him. She made him into the man he thought he'd left behind. The passionate, angry teenager, who'd lost his head, given in to rage. Desperate for something he didn't have a name for from the man who was supposed to have given him more than just pain.

Connor smiled and the reflection in the window in front of him showed him it wasn't a pleasant one. No, he'd left that furious, needy boy behind. And if he kept believing hard enough, that perfect shell would become part of him and there would be no division whatsoever.

"Of *course* you were glad he was dead," Victoria said fiercely. "He hurt you and he hurt your mother. That doesn't make you a murderer, you should know that."

"And yet a man is still dead. And I'm still glad."

"You want to punish yourself? Is that what this is all about?"

"You can't escape justice, Victoria. Or at least, you shouldn't be able to."

"Connor—"

"What?" He turned around and tried to tell himself he didn't regret the loss of warmth as her hand slipped from between his shoulder blades. "You have your explanation. What more do you want?"

There was a crease between her brows and the look in her eyes was something he didn't want to name because he thought if he did, the shell would crack. "Why didn't you tell me about this?"

"Why do you think? Did you really want to know your perfect husband killed someone once?" She opened her mouth to reply, but he kept going. "Besides, you're a fine one to talk. Why should I tell you about my father when you never breathed a word to me about the daughter you put up for adoption?"

Her jaw went tight, her arms now folded across her breasts. The hem of his shirt only barely covered the soft curls of her sex and if she moved, he'd be able to see, he was sure of it. Sick fuck that he was, to be thinking of that now.

Abruptly she looked away from him and only now did he see how the color had leeched from her skin. "Well," she said. "I guess neither of us is perfect after all. What a terrible shock."

He could feel something on the other side of the barrier he'd erected between himself and the kid he'd been. Something hungry and desperate pressing against it, clawing to get through. Wanting something from her like he'd wanted something from his father. Something he'd never gotten.

It made cold crawl through his veins.

Perhaps it was time he stopped indulging himself, at least for tonight. He had defenses to shore up, a wall to rebuild.

"Good thing I'll be signing the divorce papers at the end of this week then." His voice was icy. "Perhaps it's time you left, Victoria. I really think it would be for the best."

Her head turned, her gaze coming to his. "I thought neither of us would be running away tonight?"

"Oh and you're happy to spend it with someone like me?"

"What do you mean someone like you?"

The hungry thing battered against the wall, pushing, wanting out. "A killer."

"Why do you keep saying that? What do you expect me to do? Run screaming from the room?"

"Don't you think that's the wisest course of action?"

"I'm not afraid of you, Connor. I never have been."

"Why not?" he demanded, suddenly needing to know. "Because you should be. You should be fucking terrified."

And something in her face changed, an intensity of focus. "In case you lose your head and kill me too?"

"Jesus Christ, this is not a joke, Victoria."

"Do you see me laughing?" The look in her eyes pierced him. "From the moment I asked you to sign those papers, you've been angry. In fact you've been furious this whole week. And not once, not for one single second, have I ever been afraid of you or your anger." The certainty in her voice made that hungry desperate thing tremble. Made it yearn. It wanted her certainty. It wanted to believe it.

But no. What kind of man had no regrets about killing his father?

"What about you?" he said in a graceless change of subject. "I still don't know what happened with you."

She blinked then waved a hand. "I slept with a boy at a school dance. I lost my virginity and then had the bad luck to fall pregnant. He didn't want anything to do with me and my parents thought it would be best if I gave up the baby. They were right. So I did. What more do you want to know?"

It felt much safer not to have the focus on him, allowed him to beat back that hungry emotion, not let it get the upper hand.

"So it was as easy as that, was it?" He knew it hadn't been—she wouldn't have kept it from him all these years if it had. But the way she'd said it...as if it had happened to someone else.

She flushed. "No, of course it wasn't. But I had no choice."

"We always have choice, Victoria."

Something sparked in her eyes and he knew what it was because he was better at reading her now. Pain. "In that case I made the best choice for Jessica. The father didn't want either her or me, and I was only sixteen. My parents worked two jobs each to pay for my schooling and they'd sacrificed so much. I couldn't support her by myself and I couldn't ask my parents to help either, not after what they'd already done for me. Giving her to a family who could afford to bring her up was the best choice."

She never spoke about her family in the same way he'd never spoken about his. He'd only met her parents once, when they'd gotten married, but not since. They didn't have much to say, a quiet reserved couple who'd nevertheless seemed very pleasant. His ideal kind of parents in many ways, which had only cemented his opinion he'd made the right choice in marrying Victoria.

But for all that, she didn't speak of them and she didn't ask them to visit. From time to time she'd go down south to Wellington where they lived to visit them, but that was all.

He'd never bothered to ask why they never came here. Perhaps there was a reason. And that pain in her eyes had something to do with it.

"It might have been the best choice," he said quietly. "But was it *your* choice?"

Another flicker in her eyes. "Yes, of course it was my choice. I wanted what was best for her."

"Then why do you look like you're in pain?"

Her chin lifted. "I'm not."

"And yet you won't contact her."

"No. I told you, she didn't leave any details. If she'd wanted contact she would have said. Now can we leave the subject?"

"That's an excuse, Victoria. And you know it."

The pain in her eyes flared, changed. Became hot. Turning into anger. She took a couple of steps forward suddenly, closing the distance between them a little. "So, what? You have no excuses for your behavior? Your whole career is a crusade, Connor. And I used to think it was merely because you were passionate about the law. But it's not, is it? You're trying to atone. You're looking for people to punish because you never were."

Of course she was right. And he knew that. He'd always known it. "What's your point?"

"My point is that's an excuse as much as mine is. You hide behind your crusade, your reputation. Your whole, perfect, respectable life. And the fact is you're still hiding now." She took another step toward him. "You think I don't see the anger in your eyes? You try to pretend it isn't there, but it is. And it's been there for years." One more step, until she was only inches away, all dark-eyed heat and vibrant life. "Why are you so angry, Connor? Why are you still so angry with your father?"

It had all suddenly made sense as he'd confessed what he'd done. Telling her about his father and the violence he'd endured at the man's hands. It had been when he'd told her about his mother, about his father standing over her, the searing blue flame of rage burning so brightly in his eyes she would have been blind not to see it.

But there was something else behind that anger. Something he'd tried to mask, yet she'd seen it anyway. Anguish and a complex kind of betrayal. And no wonder. A father was supposed to love and protect his family not hurt them.

Connor was still shirtless, his broad chest rising and falling fast and hard. The tension in him was obvious in the flex and release of all those impressive muscles, though he didn't move an inch.

She could sense all that rage behind those cold eyes, locked away like he locked all the rest of his emotions away. Before she'd seen him in court, she'd used to think he didn't have any, that he was as passionless as she'd wanted to be. But of course he wasn't. He had emotions like everyone else. He just hid them better, like he hid his terrible secret.

Well, she didn't want him hiding them anymore. It was bad enough him seeing through her own paltry excuses when it came to Jessica. Seeing the guilt she thought she'd hidden so well herself. And beyond that, the fear she didn't let herself think about.

No, she wasn't going to be the only one with all her insides out on display. It was his turn now.

"What makes you think it's got anything to do with him?" His words were careful, measured. And yet the look on his face was not.

"I saw the way you looked when you told me about him. What

didn't he do, Connor? What didn't he give you that you wanted?"

Bright blue flared in his eyes. "Nothing." He virtually spat the word. "I wanted nothing from that fucker!"

But she knew that anger. And she knew the deeper, more complicated emotion behind it because it was the same thing she'd wanted from her own parents. The thing they wouldn't give her without conditions. Because nothing she did was worth the sacrifices they'd made for her and she wasn't enough on her own.

"Yes, you did. You wanted him to love you." She raised a hand to his face because she couldn't help herself.

Only to have his fingers lock around her wrist. "Don't touch me," he said roughly.

She ignored him. "But he didn't, did he? He didn't do what a father was supposed to do. And that's why you're angry. That's what's eating you up inside. Why did he do those things to you? What was wrong with you that made him hate you so much?"

His fingers tightened impossibly, making the bones of her wrist ache. But she didn't flinch, only stared into his face.

"No," he said in a voice like sand and gravel. "The problem wasn't that he hated me, Victoria. The problem was that he *loved* me."

She blinked, not understanding.

"That was love," Connor went on in his rough, grinding, menacing voice. "That was how he showed it. He hurt me because he loved me, that's what he told me every single day. And he wanted me to be hard because he wanted me to take over his goddamned fucking business!" His fingers tightened even more, making her gasp. "I used to wonder, what the hell I did to make him love me so very much. And it wasn't until I was standing over him, laying my fists into him that I knew what it was."

He was breathing faster, a stain of red on each high cheekbone, his eyes glittering. "There was something of him in me, Victoria. That's what he saw. He saw himself. And that's why he loved me."

There was so much rage in his face. Yet it wasn't that which made her ache but what lay behind it. A kind of bleak acceptance. As if he believed it himself.

"No," she said forcefully, ignoring the tight grip on her wrist. "That's bullshit, Connor Blake."

"It's not bullshit! I beat him into unconsciousness. And I fucking loved it. I was glad when he died. And I'd do it again if the opportunity provided itself. That's my father, Victoria. Violence and anger. That's all he was and that's all I was too."

She understood it now, his earlier insistence she should be afraid of him. Because he *did* believe it. And he was afraid too.

"No," she repeated, stepping right up to him so his furious gaze inches from her own. Putting all the conviction she had into her voice. The fear in his eyes, the acceptance. It wasn't right. He wasn't that man and he never would be. "What you were was an eighteen-year-old-boy fighting for your mother's life. You *saved* her for God's sake. Because you know how those cases go, Connor, you *know*. You've seen them in your own damn courtroom. There's the restraining order that never works, the promises he'll change and never touch her again. And then one day she's dead because those kinds of bastards don't change, no matter what they say."

He stared at her, breathing hard. Fast. "But there's always a choice, don't you see? I could have stopped. And I didn't."

His grip was like iron on her wrist, but she didn't care. "You had *no* choice," she insisted fiercely, willing him to believe it. "You were fighting a war. And in war there are casualties. Live by the sword, die by the sword. Remember? That's not a reminder for you to live by, that should be your father's bloody epitaph!"

He let her go, dropping her wrist as if she'd burned him. "What the hell would you know about war? About violence? About fucking choice?"

Her wrist ached but she let her arm hang down, made no move to soothe it. "I don't know anything about war or violence. But I know what it's like to have a choice in front of you, believe me. And I know how hard it is to make it. That's why your father died. Because you didn't have time to make one. It was survival, that's all it was."

"So you think I'm some kind of glorified...soldier?" There was a savage expression on his face now. "That I did something noble by taking him out?"

But she wasn't having any of that. "Weren't you? Isn't the world a better place now he's not in it?"

"It was a life, Victoria. A fucking life. It doesn't matter whether the world is better or not."

"Yes, and I'm sure your mother would agree." The words fell into a crashing silence. It was a low blow, but she wasn't sorry. She had to get him to listen somehow.

The savagery in his expression flared. "Stop it!" His voice was guttural, raw. "Stop making this okay. Stop pushing me. Don't you understand? I've spent the last twenty years keeping myself under control, making sure I never lose it like I lost it with Dad. And I was damn well succeeding until you turned up wanting those fucking papers signed!"

Shock wound through her. "What do you mean?"

"I always wanted you. Right from the moment I first saw you at the law school ball. You were so cool and contained, and I wanted a piece of that. I wanted to know how you managed it." And this time it was he who took a step forward, the heat coming off him like the sun at midday. "I learned from you, Victoria. How to keep it all locked down. How not to want. And you made it so fucking easy because you never wanted anything from me. You never seemed to want anything at all. Until that letter came and I saw what you'd been hiding."

She couldn't look away from him, all the danger and heat in his face. Mesmerizing. He was looking at her the way he had when she'd greeted him that evening. Like she was a drug and he was an addict desperate for a fix.

"I wasn't hiding anything," she said hoarsely, not knowing whether to turn and run or stand her ground.

"Yes you were. You were hiding so much passion. I could see it in your face. It made me so fucking angry because that's *not* who you were supposed to be. So I let you go when you wanted to leave. And then you had to come back with those damn papers and I knew, I just fucking knew, that I would never, ever be free of wanting you, never be free of that anger, unless I accepted it. Unless I had you for one last week, indulging every single one of my fantasies. And then I could be done with it. Only then could I be the man I always wanted to be."

She felt herself begin to shake. Because this was a part of her fantasies too, late at night, alone in her bed with her husband just down the hall. She'd dream of him telling her these exact words: *I always wanted you.*

But in one fell swoop he'd negated it. He'd negated her.

That's not who you were supposed to be.

Hurt and anger rose up inside her like a fire, searing her. Perhaps it was true. Or perhaps he was only looking to hurt her for the way she'd pushed him. Regardless of the reasons, that didn't stop her from lifting her sore hand and slapping him hard across the face in a blow which echoed around the room.

The following silence was even more deafening.

She'd never hit anyone in her entire life and part of her, the part that wasn't shaking with hurt and rage, couldn't believe she'd done it now.

The color had drained from his face, leaving only the red mark of her hand on his skin. And the impossible gas-flame blue of his eyes, burning with such ferocity she thought she'd catch fire right then and there.

The power of that look made her even angrier. She held it, her palm stinging, her heart thundering. "So all of this is my fault?" she demanded hoarsely. "*I'm* the problem? Because I wasn't who you wanted me to be?"

There was an aura of leashed violence all around him, of menace. He closed the distance between them, staring at her like he expected her to back away. But to hell with that. She wasn't going anywhere.

"No," he said roughly, now only bare inches from her, the pressure of his emotions like a physical force. "I wanted reserved and contained. That's why I married you. But you weren't either of those things up in the bar that night. With Raphael. You were so fucking sexy and you did everything I wanted. And you just made it worse." He reached for her, his arm like a steel bar around her waist, bringing her up against him. So suddenly she had to put her hands out, palms against his chest to steady herself. "This is not who I am, Victoria. This is not who I want to be. Angry and out of control and wanting you all the fucking time. But I can't seem to be anything else when I'm around you and yes, it's your fault."

He buried one hand in her hair, dragging her head back, exposing her throat, and she found herself panting. Shaking with rage and so much desire. It wasn't what she wanted either and yet here it was. "What about you, lawyer man?" she demanded, bracing her palms flat on his chest. "If you want to talk about blame, you're nothing like you were supposed to be either."

"What the hell are you talking about?" His fingers tightened.

Jesus, her voice was shaking now too. "I wanted cold. I wanted passionless, I wanted safe. But then I saw you in the courtroom and you were none of those things." She pulled against his hold on her hair, part of her relishing the prickles of pain when he didn't release her. "You were all anger and passion, and hunger. There was a goddamned warrior hiding inside of you and I didn't even know it. But that's not even the worst part." Her eyes prickled, unexpected, unwanted tears coming from where she had no idea. "The worst part was realizing I wanted all those things. And you'd been keeping them from me."

He took a breath, she could hear it. "You know why—"

"Oh yes, I know why. You kept them from me because you're too damn stupid to understand you're nothing like your father and you never will be!"

He stared at her, the pulse at the base of his throat beating fast. His fingers were knotted painfully in her hair but she ignored them, all her concentration on the hard glitter of his eyes and the singing tension she felt in his body.

"You don't want that man, Victoria," he said finally, his voice hoarse. "You really don't."

"Don't tell me what I don't want." She blinked away the tears. Hard. "I'm not interested in the man you're trying to be. I want the man you're trying to hide. That's what I've always wanted." And then, in a sudden rush. "God, let's be ourselves for once in our bloody lives!"

He gave her another long, intense look. Then the breath escaped him, a ragged, harsh sound. "I'm not …sure I know how."

She swallowed, her throat aching. "You do, Connor. Just be the man you've been every night this week."

His chest heaved, a wild light in his eyes. "And then we end it. We take our week and when it's over we don't look back. We don't ever fucking look back."

He was right. In so many ways he was right. Two days left to be themselves and then they could move on. Then they could be the people they were supposed to be.

She didn't know why that made her feel so desperate. "Okay," she agreed thickly, telling herself as well as him. "No looking back."

He only hesitated for a moment before bending his head and covering her mouth. It was a hard, insistent, devouring kiss. And she returned it, just as hard, just as insistent. She sank her hands into his hair the way she'd done at the dinner table, curling her fingers in the silky strands, gripping him tightly as he gripped her.

There was a fever in the kiss that hadn't been there before. Hunger with a raw edge. The knowledge that this was all there would ever be for either of them. This was all they could have of one another.

And it would have to be enough.

Connor broke the kiss abruptly then with one forceful movement, he pulled the business shirt she wore off her, leaving her naked. Before she could move, she found herself turned around and propelled across the room to the bed, shoved face-down onto it. She put her palms on the mattress, preparing to lever herself up, only to feel his hand at the small of her back, pinning her down.

"You don't want the lawyer?" Connor hissed in her ear. "You may regret it."

His other hand, warm and sure, moved over the curve of her butt, then squeezed. Hard. She kicked out at him, panting, only to feel his thumb slide between her buttocks, circling then pressing down on the sensitive opening there.

She gasped, turning her head on the sheets as a wave of heat engulfed her. She'd never had anyone touch her there and now he was…he was…

"Connor!" His name burst from her as his thumb pressed harder, pushing inside her. "Ah, God…" Her fingers curled in the sheets, the filthy pleasure of the sensation stealing the air from her lungs.

"You like that, don't you?" His voice was a whisper, the warmth of his breath stealing over her bare shoulder. "My thumb here. But you're such a dirty little girl I think you'd prefer my cock instead. In fact, I think you'd love to have my cock there."

Victoria screwed her eyes shut, his thumb moving gently, in stark contrast to the rough words and the weight of his palm pressing in the small of her back. She could hardly breathe as sensation began to pull tight, a vicious, brutal kind of climax waiting for her.

This was wrong. This was dirty. She loved it. And she wanted more.

"Don't be coy," she panted, shoving herself back against his hand. "Tell me where you want to put your cock."

There was a pause, a little flare of satisfaction curling inside her as she realized she'd surprised him. Then unexpectedly he laughed, a husky, wholly sexual sound that shivered over her like a caress. It was almost shocking. She'd never heard him laugh like that.

"Christ, you're amazing." His lips brushed against her ear, his teeth closing down on her earlobe in a hard nip. "I want to put my cock in your ass, you sexy bitch. That explicit enough for you?"

He moved his thumb again, as if to emphasize the point and she bit back a groan. "So stop talking about it and do it. Or is lawyer Connor getting in the way again?"

The weight on her back disappeared, his arm coming down near her head as he braced himself. "I don't want to hurt you." There was a rough need in his voice and a note of concern that had her throat tightening.

"That didn't appear to bother you when you fucked me up against the wall downstairs," she pointed out.

"This is different. We've never done this before."

"We hadn't done it up against a wall before either but that didn't stop us." It was nice he'd thought of her, that her comfort mattered to him. But then he had right the way through their little arrangement, hadn't he? Rearranging her clothes. Cooking her dinner. Giving her space when she needed it. And pushing her, all the time pushing her whether he knew it or not, to be herself.

The tightness in her throat moved down into her chest.

"Are you sure?" His breath feathered over her nape.

She was shivering and it wasn't anything to do with the sex.

You fall for him and this will be the end of you. The end of the person you want to be.

There would be no more cool. No more reserve. No more containment. Nothing to hide behind anymore.

Fear gripped her, clutching at her throat so tight she could hardly breathe.

"We don't have to, Victoria," he said quietly, misinterpreting her hesitation and shifting a little, withdrawing his thumb from her. "There's no pressure."

She could run right now. Run right out of this house and never come back. She'd only miss out on two more days.

You promised him you wouldn't run.

She swallowed and didn't move. Because it wasn't only her promise that held her still. She wanted the freedom they'd only just discovered. Freedom from the secrets, from the excuses, from each other's expectations. She wanted the passion, the desire and the hunger. The giving over of herself to sensation, and to hell with the consequences. She wanted one last taste before they went back to their separate lives.

And that was stronger by far than her fear.

Which meant she'd just have to not fall for him.

"Why?" she asked thickly, wanting to goad him. "Don't tell me you're scared of a little butt sex, lawyer man?"

"Jesus, you do love playing with fire." He nipped her ear again. "Okay then, you asked for it. Now stay exactly like that. I have to go get a couple of things."

He pushed himself away, the warmth of his body disappearing.

Victoria kept her eyes shut, her heartbeat thundering in her ears. She could hear his footsteps moving over to the nightstand and a drawer being pulled out then pushed back in again. The sound of him returning.

Her fingers curled tighter in the sheet as anticipation began to build. And when he finally touched her she shivered all over because it wasn't where she expected, a light finger trailing down the length of her spine. She sighed then felt his thumb, slippery with a cold liquid that must have been lube, push between her buttocks again, easing inside her, beginning to work the liquid into her exquisitely sensitive opening.

Goose bumps broke out all over her skin and she gasped at the sensation, that wicked, vicious pleasure starting to build. A distant part of her wanted to fight it, wanted to hold out against it like it was a line she couldn't cross. But she was through with that part of herself. She was going to give in, revel in the sensation, take the pleasure and run with it because it wouldn't happen again. She couldn't do this with another man. She wouldn't be able to do this with *any* other men. Only Connor.

You're falling. Don't.

The breath escaped her in a rush, her eyes opening. Directly beside the bed were the doors of the closet. The ones closest to the head of the bed weren't mirrored but the ones toward the end were. And she could see him standing behind her. She could see the moment when he reached out and stroked her spine while he worked his thumb, the look on his face fierce with hunger, and something else she couldn't read.

And the pleasure grew, twined with a tight, needy sensation in her chest.

There was tenderness in the touch on her spine and yet a hard, insistent pressure from his thumb, the combination of both making her want to squirm against his hand to get herself off and yet burst into tears at the same time.

She closed her eyes against the sight, fighting the tightness in her chest. Pushing herself against his probing thumb, wanting that sensation instead.

But his hand came down hard on one buttock, making her jerk at the unexpected smack. "Stop," he ordered sharply. "Keep still otherwise you won't get what you want, greedy girl."

God, she wanted to push that boundary too, explore that sensation as well, because it too was better than the feeling behind her ribs. The ache at the back of her throat.

But before she could make the decision, she heard a crinkle of foil and felt him gently part her buttocks. And then the head of his cock was pressing against her ass. She shuddered at the sensation of pressure. He pushed a little harder, the tight ring of muscle giving and unexpected tears started behind her eyes. She'd been expecting pain but still.

"You okay?" he asked thickly. "Shall I stop? Fuck, you're so tight."

Perhaps he should. Perhaps this was too much.

She opened her eyes again, her gaze drawn helplessly to the reflection in the mirror. His hands were gripping her hips, his tall, broad figure positioned behind her and there was something unbearably erotic about the look on his face. It was all tension and hunger, desire and desperation. Yet all tightly leashed. Holding himself back. For her.

Don't fall. Don't.

No, of course she wouldn't. And she was letting the emotions get to her, rather than the physical aspect of the sex. Which meant she needed to go through with this, prove to herself she was stronger. Besides, they'd already crossed so many lines, what was one more? There was only forward from this moment. And once it was over, once they'd come out the other side of wherever this was going, they'd both finally be free.

"Keep going," she said hoarsely.

So he did. Gently. Rocking into her in short, slow movements. Deepening his penetration by increments. And she kept her gaze on his face, watching mesmerized as the tension in it is pulled even tighter.

There wasn't so much pain now, only pressure. An intense stretching sensation that made her tremble, another wave of heat going through her. She felt full and at the same time empty. The pleasure deep and yet not enough.

"C-Connor." His name escaped without her permission and his gaze shifted, found hers in the mirror. Held.

Her throat ached. She wanted to look away, close her eyes, but she couldn't seem to do so.

Falling...

He didn't speak, his eyes locked with hers, his hips moving, pushing deeper and deeper. There were no more dirty words, no more dirty names. Only an intimacy that made her feel utterly defenseless, even more exposed than she had been when he'd watched her with Raphael.

"Connor," she said again, not really knowing whether she wanted him to stop or to look away, only that she needed to say his name.

Again, he didn't reply. He was all the way inside her now, a heavy, insistent pressure, pausing only to slide one arm around her waist and hold her hard against him.

She found she was panting, trembling, completely caught by the intensity of his gaze.

He began to move again, the push of his hips picking up speed, becoming a little more forceful. Watching her in the mirror. Seeing her. And she wanted to tell him to look away, anything so he wouldn't see the pleasure she was getting from this. The way the sensation was breaking her apart.

"Victoria," he said roughly and she felt his other hand move against her stomach, sliding down between her thighs, finding the tight little bud of her clit. Circling it. Electricity fired through her in an intense, hard burst.

Victoria. Not all those erotic, exciting words he'd called her before. Words she could hide behind, masks she could wear for a while and put down again afterwards.

Only her name. Her real name.

Falling so hard...

"No," she gasped as his circling fingers moved lower, stroking the folds of her sex.

"Yes." Two fingers slid inside her, thrusting in time with the push of his cock. His gaze unwavering, locked on hers. "You're my Victoria. My dirty, beautiful, sexy Victoria."

And much to her horror, she felt her eyes fill with tears again, the wild, raw pleasure turning inside her. Unstoppable. Inexorable.

"I'm not." Her voice was a thread, a thin whisper of sound.

"You are." He twisted his fingers, his eyes glittering in the dim light of the room, the expression on his face savage with desire. "You're mine, Victoria. Mine." And he brushed his thumb over her clit.

The orgasm exploded through her, a supernova of pure sensation, electrifying her, a scream tearing from her throat. And still she couldn't look away from him, every nerve ending igniting, tears overflowing and running down her cheeks, sobs catching her throat. Watching the blue of his eyes become brilliant, his expression agonized as his rhythm changed, became jerky. A growling roar escaped him, the unguarded pleasure in his face incandescent.

It was only then she was able to tear her gaze away, burying her hot cheeks in the cool cotton of the pillowcase.

She'd been right to be afraid. He'd broken her. Systematically laid waste to the person she was trying to be, reducing her to nothing but shattered pieces.

Fallen.

And she had no idea how she was going to rebuild herself again.

Chapter Eleven

Connor woke at his usual time of six a.m., way earlier than he would have liked, but the irritation of that was mitigated by the fact that when he turned his head, there was a naked woman sprawled on the bed beside him. And not just any naked woman. Victoria.

She was lying on her stomach, her head buried in the pillow, very firmly asleep. The sheet had slipped off her, revealing long limbs and delicious curves, a black storm of curls against the white cotton of the pillowcase.

He turned on his side, studying her for a long moment. He couldn't remember the last time they'd slept in the same bed, still less woken up together. Certainly he'd never woken up to find her naked beside him.

An overwhelming sense of satisfaction settled inside him and he couldn't help reaching out to trail his fingers over the smooth curve of her back.

He felt…strangely hollow. But this time the feeling was a good one. As if something that had turned poisonous had been drained away, leaving an empty, clean sort of feeling.

Perhaps it was just the sex, but he didn't think so. There was more to it than that. Certainly the sex between them had uncovered things, unlocked parts of themselves they'd never known existed. And those parts seem to fit together very well.

They fit perfectly.

Especially last night. And it hadn't been in the tight feel of her ass around his cock, or the dirty fantasy he'd imagined finally becoming reality. It was in the conviction in her voice when she'd told him what he'd done to his father was a matter of survival, his and his mother's. That he hadn't had a choice. The utter certainty of it had had him protesting purely because he wanted to believe her so very badly and just couldn't let himself.

It had also been in the look in her eyes as he'd met her gaze in the mirror. An intense and complicated look. Because behind the desire and pleasure in her face had been what looked like fear. And longing. A wordless question demanding an answer. So he'd given it.

Mine. You're mine, Victoria.

He'd never been possessive but in that moment he'd felt it so strongly he hadn't been able to keep quiet. And not just for her sexy body and her uninhibited passion. He also wanted her belief in him, her conviction, and her complete certainty he was not the man he was secretly afraid he was. No one else had ever given him that and he didn't want to share it.

She'd showed that side of herself to no one else but him. Even with Raphael, she hadn't been as naked as she'd been last night with him.

And you don't want her being naked like that with anyone else but you.

He let out a breath, his fingers trailing over the curve of her ass as he accepted the truth of it. No, he didn't and that was a problem when in a couple of days all of this would be over and they would both be free to go on with their lives.

You also don't want it to be over.

Connor's hand stilled in the small of her back, the warmth of her skin against his palm. Something heavy shifted inside his chest. Knowledge.

Certainty.

No, he didn't want it to be over. Last night they'd crossed a line in more ways than one. In sharing their secrets and then their bodies, they'd been themselves.

And she'd accepted him. The man he'd been hiding, the man he was behind the shell that was Connor Blake, lawyer. More than accepted him, she'd wanted him.

And he wanted her, the woman he'd uncovered. Not just to have in his bed, but to get to know. Her thoughts and desires, her dreams.

But he only had one more night left and that wasn't enough for someone as complicated and fascinating as Victoria. He needed longer. Another week. A month. Maybe even a year.

There will never be enough time.

His breath caught and abruptly he turned and sat up, swinging his legs over the side of the bed, pausing a moment.

No, he didn't know how long it would take to get enough of Victoria. But one thing he was sure of, one more night wasn't going to cut it. He wanted more. He wanted longer.

Pushing himself off the bed, he headed toward the shower, still thinking.

The time for running away from what was happening between them was over. He needed to talk to her. Lay out what he wanted. He had no guarantees she would feel the same way, of course, especially considering she was planning on leaving the country. But maybe he could get her to put it off. Because surely this was worth it?

Once he was showered and dressed for work, he headed down to the kitchen and pulled some bacon and eggs from the fridge. Protein for breakfast was exactly what they both needed for this kind of discussion.

He had coffee brewing on the stove and was halfway through cooking the eggs and bacon when Victoria appeared in the doorway. Unfortunately she was not wearing his shirt the way she had the night before, but the clothes she'd arrived in last night, the shirt and blouse looking a little worse for wear, her hair loose down her back. Not Victoria-the-lawyer, and yet not dirty-girl-Victoria either. More like a pretty damn sexy combination of the two.

"Why don't you sit down?" he said, gesturing to the breakfast bar. "I'll get you some coffee while the eggs cook."

"It's okay." Her voice was cool. "I'll pick up a coffee on the way to work. I have to go home to get changed anyway." There was a slightly guarded look in her eyes, one he didn't like, that made his heart tighten behind his ribs.

"It's one coffee, Victoria. Stay. I have something I want to discuss."

She leaned against the doorframe and he experienced a sudden, weird sense of dislocation. Last night she'd leaned against that doorframe in nothing but one of his business shirts. And before that, years before, as his wife, he'd seen her do the same thing, all cool and reserved, stopping to say goodbye as she went off to work. Or saying hello as she arrived home.

Now this woman was there, in the doorway. A mixture of the wild, passionate woman who'd screamed into the mattress the night before and the contained and brilliant lawyer he'd married. The woman who'd gotten all his secrets out of him. Who hadn't been afraid.

"Discuss what?" she said. "I don't want to be late for work."

The sharp, unexpected edges of disappointment cut into him, like the teeth of a newly sharpened saw. Because he could see already the guarded look in her eyes wasn't changing. That, if possible, it was becoming even more guarded, even more wary. She was protecting herself. Withdrawing herself from him.

Well, too bad. He'd stayed silent, kept quiet for too many years and now the time for silence was over. They had to be honest with each other if there was to be any hope for them.

And he wanted there to be hope. Because for perhaps for the first time in years, he had something he wanted more than justice.

He flicked the gas element off and dropped the spatula onto the counter with a clatter. Turned to face her. "Screw work. This is more important."

She stared at him for a long time, a complicated expression in her dark eyes. One he couldn't read for the life of him. "What is more important?"

"This. Us. What happened last night."

"What do you mean what happened last night?"

"You know what I'm talking about. We shared something, Victoria. Not just our secrets and not just our dirty little fantasies. We shared ourselves with each other in a way we haven't before. Don't you think that's important?"

Her gaze flickered and she shifted against the doorframe. "I'm not quite sure what you're getting at."

She didn't want to understand, he realized. She didn't want to know. Fine. He'd spell it out for her so they were both utterly clear.

"I don't want this to be over at the end of the week," he said flatly. "We have something between us we've never had before and I want more of it. I want to explore it, see where it takes us."

She blinked then looked away from him, down at the floor, her hands clasped in front of her. "I see."

"Good. Does that mean you agree?"

Her attention remained on the floor and she was silent a long moment. Then abruptly she lifted her head. "So you really think after a few days of sex I'd be willing to give up my position in London, my travel plans, my entire future, to stay here and 'explore' more sex with you?" There was a stain of red along her cheekbones and a spark gleamed in her dark eyes. Anger.

"I'm not asking you to give up anything. But maybe you might want to postpone it."

"Are you completely out of your mind?"

"No, I'm not. In fact, for the first time in five fucking years I'm actually thinking clearly for once."

"Well, good for you. But I'm afraid I'm going to have to refuse. You wanted a week and that's what I'm giving you. No more. So if you'll excuse me, I'd better get—"

"Don't be a fucking coward, Victoria," he interrupted, anger and disappointment beginning to bite. And this time he didn't fight them. He let them loose. "You always run away when things get tough and I get it, you're protecting yourself. But you don't need to do that anymore, not with me. Haven't we gotten beyond that?"

She didn't reply immediately, staring at him. Then she pushed herself away from the doorframe, standing in the doorway like she was about to take flight. "What do you seriously expect to have happen from this 'exploration', Connor?" she demanded. "You want to go back to our marriage? Is that it?"

"If you mean what we had before, then Christ, no. I don't." He took a step toward her. "I want what we had this week. I want the good parts of our marriage and the passion as well." Another step, holding her gaze.

"I want what I saw in your eyes when you looked at me in the mirror last night." The same look Lily had given Kahu. Finally, finally. As if he'd been the only person in her entire universe…

The hectic color had faded from her face, leaving her pale, her eyes even darker. "I don't know what you saw in the mirror last night. We had sex. That's all. And a couple of extra truths thrown in for good measure is not a basis to go building anything on, still less rebuilding a marriage already broken before we even tied the knot."

Of course she would deny it. That's what she did when she felt threatened, he knew that now. But still the deep surge of anger that went through him caught him off guard. "Bull*shit*, Victoria. It wasn't just about the sex and you know it."

"But that's just it. I *don't* know it." Her chin lifted. "So why don't you tell me what you think it's all about?"

He closed the distance between them, for once not thinking, only acting. And when he reached her, he took her proud, determined chin in his hand, tilting her head back so she could look into his eyes. So she could see. "It's about us, Victoria. Being real with each other. Being ourselves for the first time in five fucking years the way you said last night. No secrets. No masks. And no fear." He searched her face, looking deep into her guarded brown eyes. "Don't you want that? Because I do. I want it so goddamned much it hurts." He knew as soon as he said it that it was true. He wanted it. He wanted her. Right down to his bones, to his soul.

More than he wanted anything else. More than atonement or absolution or forgiveness for his sins. More than he wanted to protect himself and keep himself safe.

She was more important than any of that and what they'd discovered together, what they could be together, was worth paying any price for.

And it was strange how, understanding that, the anger just flowed out of him, leaching away. A calm settling down inside him he hadn't felt for years, if ever. He knew what he wanted now. What he had to fight for.

Last night he'd told her everything and she hadn't run. More than that. She'd believed he wasn't what he'd always thought, what he'd always feared. A violent, angry man, just like his father. She'd called what he'd done survival. A war. And you didn't have a choice with a war. You only had to fight.

Well, now it was time for another fight. Another battle. But this time it wouldn't be survival he'd be fighting for, it would be her. Down to the last of his strength.

"Victoria," he said softly, releasing her chin, his hand dropping to where hers were, clasped together over her stomach. "Let's try this. Let's see where it takes us. Let's try again."

She was breathing fast, her jaw tight, the expression in her eyes almost anguished. "Connor...I..."

He took one of her hands in his, twining his fingers through hers and holding on. "Please."

Her mouth closed and for a second she was still. Then slowly and with great care she extracted her fingers from his grip. "I'm sorry. I can't."

The loss of her warmth was a shadow over the sun, an ache in his heart. "Why not?"

Unexpectedly her guarded look crumbled, and he saw the sheen of tears in her eyes. "Because I'm not what you want. I'm not who you want. I never have been. And I never will be."

He wanted to touch her then, wanted to take her in his arms. Show her she was exactly what he wanted. Only sex wasn't going to solve this one. It had been the catalyst that had brought them to this point. But it wouldn't take them beyond it. For that, there needed to be more.

There has to be love.

The emotion he'd always dreaded, clouded by violence and the sound of his father's shouts, his mother's screams, the smack of a fist into unprotected flesh. He'd never wanted love, never sought it. But he knew in that moment that's what he'd seen in her eyes last night. That's what he'd felt in his heart.

"You are what I want," he said, the rough edge of emotion creeping into his voice and he let it. "You're exactly what I want."

She shook her head as if denying it. "No. You want someone else, Connor. A different woman. And I'm not her."

It hurt. It goddamn hurt. Because he knew what he saw in her, he knew what she was. "You *are* her, Victoria. That's who you are inside. Why can't you see that?"

Her expression closed up. "You don't understand. I don't *want* to be her. I don't *want* to have anything to do with her." Acid edged her words, a bitter self-loathing he'd never heard before. "*She* walked away from her baby. *She* walked away from her own child. And all because she was trying to live up to some impossible set of expectations. Trying to make her parents' sacrifice worth it. Who would ever want anything to do with a woman like that?"

There was pain in her face, despite her shuttered look. And he understood, finally, that her scars ran just as deep as his. "I would," he said, quiet and sure.

Her throat moved, the pain in her eyes spreading outwards. "Why? What the hell do you see in her?"

"Because she's in pain. Because she wants forgiveness. Because she cares. Just the same as I do."

"She doesn't want any of those things."

"I think she wants love."

She went even paler, turning away from him. "No. You're wrong. She wants love the least of all."

"Victoria—"

"Goodbye, Connor," she said, turning her back on him. "Thanks for everything."

Then she began to walk away.

"That's your answer to everything, isn't it?" he said, not raising his voice, making it a challenge. "You run away when it gets difficult. When it gets painful. When you're scared. That's what you've done for the past five years and you're still doing it now."

She paused, but didn't turn. "I have to protect myself somehow."

"From what? From me?"

She only shook her head, not answering him, beginning to walk again.

"I'm not running, Victoria." He said it quietly but loud enough she heard, he knew she did. "I'm going to fight for this. I'm going to fight for you."

She reached the front door and pulled it open.

"You'll never get your divorce," Connor said. "I'm never going to let you go."

And she shut it behind her.

That was fine. She could run away again, but it would be for the last time. Because he was done with letting her walk away from him.

Last night she'd showed him the strength of her conviction. It was time she learned about his.

"What's up?"

Victoria pushed the remains of her chicken salad around on her plate. Not that it could rightly be called remains when she hadn't eaten any of it. "Nothing," she said, trying to keep her tone even. "I'm fine."

Across the table from her, Eleanor gave a disbelieving snort. "Bullshit, Vic. What's going on?"

They were having lunch at the Auckland Club and it had not escaped Victoria's notice that Raphael was behind the bar. She'd flushed as they'd entered and she'd spotted him, but he only nodded his head at her, his smile holding nothing but friendliness. That had eased the tension, but the sight of him also reminded her of what had happened only last week.

It reminded her of Connor.

Let's try again. Please.

"Vic. Come on."

She dropped her fork, her chest feeling empty and hollow. She didn't want to talk about it.

You run away when it gets difficult...

There was worry in Eleanor's gray eyes, a crease between her fair brows. There was no point in telling her friend about Connor. She would be leaving in a couple of weeks anyway and then it would be a moot point.

But the hollow feeling in her chest wouldn't go away. She couldn't get the image of Connor standing in the kitchen out of her head. Of the look in his eyes. No anger, only a tenderness that made her feel like she was suffocating. An expression that wasn't for her and that she didn't deserve anyway.

He didn't understand. She'd made the decision to give Jessica up. She hadn't fought. She'd done what she was told. She'd obeyed her parents to make them happy. Because that's what she always did, struggling to live up to their vaunted ideas about what they wanted for her. Because she loved them.

Jesus, it all came back to that, didn't it? Love. That demanded too many sacrifices. Too many parts of your soul. A soul already broken into pieces the day she'd handed over her daughter to the nurse in the hospital.

She didn't have much of her soul left. She couldn't hand the rest over to Connor just like that.

He'd accused her of walking away, of not fighting, and he was right. She didn't want to fight. It was easier and less painful to protect yourself, and it was much safer in the long run. She'd been doing that for too many years to stop suddenly now.

"Vic," Eleanor said again. "You look miserable. And I'm worried about you."

Victoria looked at her salad, her appetite completely gone. "I've been seeing Connor," she heard herself say, the words abrupt and flat. "We've been... Well, anyway. It's over now."

There was a shocked silence.

"You kept that quiet," Eleanor murmured.

She looked up, met her friend's steady gaze. "It was a goodbye fling type of arrangement."

"So why are you unhappy?"

"I'm not—" She stopped abruptly as Eleanor raised a skeptical brow. "All right, so I'm...sad. But it's over and done with now, like I said. And I'm leaving for London soon."

"Uh huh." Eleanor sat back in her chair, nursing a glass of rosé. There was a searching expression on her face that made Victoria uncomfortable. "So you're sad. Why?"

She forced herself to laugh, a brittle sound. "Because the sex was good."

"You can have good sex with someone else, Vic. That's usually not a reason to be sad."

"I don't want sex with someone else," she said before she could stop herself.

"Ah. Well, that's different then."

Victoria pushed her salad plate away with a sharp movement, angry with herself and with the horrible feeling in her chest that wouldn't go away.

You're afraid.

Yes, she *was* afraid. She'd made a great many sacrifices in her life and she didn't want to have to make any more. And there would be sacrifices if she wanted to be with Connor because there always were.

Such as? Giving up a passionless, loveless life?

"It's not different," she said forcefully. "I can be celibate." After all, she'd been celibate for at least two years before she and Connor had gotten it on. She could do it again. "Anyway, it's not about the sex."

"Then what is it about? You want more and he doesn't?"

"No. I'm the one who doesn't want more."

Eleanor gave her a narrow look. "Oh, so he does?"

"Yes. He wants to…try again."

"But you don't."

"No."

"Why not?"

A simple question with a not so simple answer. "It's complicated."

Eleanor gave a soft laugh. "Yeah, it always is. Apparently. But sometimes, it's actually quite simple. You either love him and want to try and make it work. Or you don't."

No, it wasn't that simple. Eleanor didn't know about Jessica or Connor's father. Didn't know about the passionless marriage she and Connor had had before. Didn't know about the passion they'd discovered between them. There was too much that was complicated. Too much that was painful.

Bullshit. She's right and you know it. You either love him and he's worth trying for. Or you don't and he's not.

Victoria's throat closed, the hollow feeling deepening into an ache. That knowledge of what she felt for him sitting in the back of her mind. A pull she couldn't deny. The same kind of pull that dragged at her whenever she thought about her daughter. Longing. Yearning for something she couldn't have. Something she didn't deserve.

His strength. His sense of fairness, of justice. His passion.

"I will fight for you..."

No one had ever fought for her. No one had ever believed in her.

Because you've never been good enough.

She stood all of a sudden, her chair scraping back loudly on the wooden floor. She had to get out, get away. Somewhere away from the thoughts going 'round and 'round in her head. From the feelings inside her stinging like salt in an open wound.

"Sorry, Ell," she said, her voice sounding strange. "I have to get back to work. I'll call you."

As she stalked out of the club, she tried to ignore the look of disappointment on Eleanor's face. And the sound of Connor's voice resounding in her head. The one that kept whispering she was running away. Easy for him to say when it was painfully obvious he'd never had a choice about the demons in his past. He'd had to fight, for his mother's life and for his own. Survival at its purest level.

But she'd had a choice. And she'd always known, deep in her heart, her choice had been a selfish one. Telling herself adoption was the right thing to do for her daughter, that it was best for Jessica. When ultimately, all it had been about what was best for *her*.

She could have fought for her baby. She could have stood up to her parents and refused to give her up. She could have carved a life out for herself and her child.

And she hadn't. She caved. Because she wanted their approval, their love, more than she'd wanted her daughter.

It was a decision she'd hate herself for making forever.

Her PA gave her a meaningful look as she came into the office. "You've got someone to see you."

Victoria didn't pause. She didn't have an appointment booked, but whoever it was would get short shrift. She wasn't in any mood to make nice. "Thanks, Estelle," she said as she passed the desk. "I'll deal with it."

But as she pushed open the door to her office, her heart just about stopped in her chest.

Connor was leaning back against her desk, his hands braced on either side of him, fingers gripping the edge.

It had only been two days since she'd walked out of his kitchen, trying to tell herself it was for the best. Only two short days. Yet as soon as his intense gaze met hers, she felt the weight of all those hours and minutes and seconds without him pile on top of her, heavy as eternity.

An absurd impulse gripped her. To fling aside her briefcase and launch herself at him. But of course she wasn't going to. Any physical contact they'd had was over and done with now. No point in going back.

"What are you doing here?" She kept her tone cool as she calmly closed the door behind her. "I wasn't expecting you."

"You should have." His sharp, perceptive gaze didn't waver. "I told you I wasn't going to let you go."

She took a slow, silent breath, trying to calm the wild beating of her heart. "I don't want you to fight for me. I didn't ask you to fight for me."

"I know you didn't. But I'm going to all the same. In fact, you would have seen me again the day you walked out, but I had a few things to do."

Carefully she placed her briefcase down on the meeting table near her desk. She wanted to keep hold of it to maintain some kind of barrier between them, but again, that would reveal too much. And she didn't want to give him any more in the way of ammunition.

"What things?"

"I had to tie up the loose ends of the case I'm dealing with now." He shifted against the desk and she tried not to notice the way the wool of his suit trousers pulled tight around his powerful thighs, or how the black belt he wore emphasized his lean hips.

Hunger turned over inside her, just as powerful, just as insistent as it had been before. As if the past few days hadn't done a thing.

You'll never stop wanting him.

"What case?" she asked, trying to drown out the voice in her head.

"A young guy who shot his father. The police are trying to bring a murder charge but we've had some evidence turn up that's going to make that impossible." He paused, staring at her. "I've passed the case on to someone else. In fact, I should never have taken it on in the first place considering the conflict of interest. But I did because you were right, it was part of my crusade." His gaze was very direct. "I've been trying to atone. And I thought I could achieve that by punishing people for their crimes. That's been the focus of my life ever since I got into law school. That's been the way I dealt with what happened to Dad." He hesitated. "But then you told me something different. You told me I was only defending myself, protecting my mother. That it was survival. And you were... Christ, Victoria, you were so damn sure. So damn certain. And I was afraid to believe you. Because what if you're wrong?"

"I'm not wrong," she said in a thick voice. She couldn't look away from him. There was something in his face that was different. An intensity that didn't come from anger this time, but from certainty. Surety.

"I know you're not. That's why I've decided I want to take that chance." He was quiet but no less certain. "I've decided to believe you. I'm not like my father and I don't have to hide or keep myself locked down." Another pause. "Because you weren't afraid of me. And if you weren't afraid, then there's no reason on earth for me to be."

Such measured, logical words. Making so much sense. And yet they cut her to shreds because there was a trust implicit in them she was sure she hadn't earned.

She glanced away, blinking away the prick of something that felt suspiciously like tears behind her eyes. "So what does that mean?"

"I can't change the past. I can't take back what I did. But I'm going to stop taking these prosecution cases and look into doing some pro-bono work for people in need instead. Do more family law stuff, I think. Domestic violence. Custody issues. I want to help people trapped in the same kind of situation I was in." His mouth turned up in a faint, self-deprecating smile. "You need passion for those kinds of cases. You need belief. And you need anger. Especially if you want to make a positive difference to their lives."

A bright spark had lit in his eyes, the one she'd seen only in the courtroom. And the hunger sank its claws deeper inside her.

"That's great," she said, toneless and brittle. "I think you'll be fantastic at it."

He didn't move, nor did he look away. "It's because of you, Victoria. You understand that, don't you? If you hadn't confronted me that night, I doubt I'd ever have taken this step."

"I only made you see what was already there." She glanced down at her watch to check the time, needing the excuse to look away from him. "Now, have you got anything else to say? I have another meeting in about ten minutes." A total lie. But she wanted him out of here.

"I also brought you something."

She looked up. "What?"

He shifted again and picked up a white envelope lying on top of her desk. "This." And handed it to her.

Victoria took it and lifted the envelope tab, sliding out the papers inside.

The divorce papers. Signed.

Her stomach lurched, an unexpected and bitter disappointment she told herself she didn't feel. "But you said you would never—"

"Give you a divorce? I know. But like I said, I've been thinking since you left. Make no mistake, Victoria. I meant what I said when I told you I would fight for you. For us. I want you. I want this and I'm going to do my damnedest to make you see that too. But I'm not going to do that by denying you what's important to you." He nodded toward the papers she held. "I've signed them like you wanted and it's up to you whether you send them. However, you're on notice right now I fully intend to seduce the hell out of you and get you to remarry me at the first opportunity."

Her throat felt thick. Her chest tight. She turned and put the papers on the meeting table, not wanting to look at them anymore. Keeping her back to him. "Thank you," she said, trying to keep her voice level. "But you only have two weeks for all of that because I'll be leaving for England."

"Oh, I'll have more than two weeks. I've decided to join you in London."

Another shock, like cold water down her back.

Victoria turned sharply. "What?"

His gaze was unflinching. "I have a lot of leave I need to use up anyway. It shouldn't be too difficult to organize."

"So you're going to hand over all your cases just like that? To follow me to London?"

"You were so certain about me, Victoria. Now it's my turn to show you how certain I am about you."

The heaviness inside her shifted, making her shiver inexplicably. "But...why?"

He pushed himself away from the desk and before she could move, he'd crossed the space between them. She found herself backed up against the table, the hard heat of him in front of her, the ferocity she'd seen so often in his eyes burning once more. But not this time from anger, but another, far more potent emotion. "Don't you think you're worth it? Don't you think you're worth fighting for?"

Something was breaking inside of her and she didn't know what it was. It frightened her. "You can't do that," she said hoarsely. "You can't give up everything for me."

"And you're avoiding the question." His voice was gentle, horribly so. "Why shouldn't I give up everything for you?" He lifted a hand, his fingers brushing her cheekbone.

And at the touch, the thing that had started to break, that was so very, very fragile after all, began to shatter, to crumble and she didn't know how to stop it.

"Connor," she whispered instead. "Please don't."

"Don't what? Don't fight for you? Don't love you?"

Her vision blurred. "You don't understand. I don't want you to love me. I don't need it."

"I thought I didn't need it either." His fingers trailed down the side of her cheek, along her jawline. Tender. Forgiving. "Turns out I do. And I think you do too."

She closed her eyes against the sudden, hot rush of tears, coming from a place in her heart she tried to tell herself wasn't there. "No. Please, no."

But he ignored that. "I think you do want it, Victoria. I think you're desperate for it. But I also think you're too afraid to take it."

She kept her eyes closed. Because it was too hard to look at him. Too hard to accept what he seemed to be offering. "I can't, Connor. I don't want to feel like nothing I do is good enough. I don't want to feel like I'm being measured and found wanting. Like there's this goal I have to reach to finally be worthy. I've been there, done that." Finally she opened her eyes and looked up at him. "I gave up a piece of myself for love. I gave up Jessica. And it nearly killed me. I can't do it again."

"But I'm not asking you to give up anything, Victoria. I just want you, exactly as you are. I want the intellectual, intelligent, brilliant woman I married. And the passionate, sexy, dirty girl I've only just discovered. All those different parts of you, I want them. I want to discover and explore them. You don't have to be anything else, anyone else, but who you already are."

A lone tear escaped one corner of her eye, trailing in a hot line down her cheek. And she opened her eyes. "Connor…" Her voice failed. It felt like she'd been hungry for so long, her needs grown so vast and complex, she couldn't even give names to them. "It's just… My parents…wanted big things from me. And they worked so hard to give me opportunities and I…" She let out a shaken breath. "I never felt equal to all the sacrifices they made. I never asked for them. I never wanted them. I just wanted… I just wanted them to love me, not give up their whole lives for me." She swallowed, hating the needy sound in her voice. "But they did and then I got pregnant. And I wanted that baby so much. So goddamn much." A deep, visceral pain twisted inside her, a pain she'd never been able to outrun no matter how hard she tried.

Connor didn't speak. He only reached to brush away the tear, his touch gentle against her skin.

"They wouldn't help me," she whispered, the touch breaking her a little more. "They said I wouldn't be able to take care of her, that she'd be better off with people who could give her the life she deserved. And they'd worked too hard to see me throw away the opportunities they'd given me." The pain twisted again, harder. "So I gave her up. And I've been telling myself over and over that was the right choice. The only one. But I always knew the choice I was making wasn't for her. It was for me." The words cracked, the pain inside leaking out.

"Victoria," he murmured. "Don't—"

But she didn't let him finish. "*I* could have fought. *I* could have said no. *I* could have kept her. But I didn't." Another tear fell down her cheek. "I was too afraid of losing what I had."

The look in his eyes was so full of understanding she could hardly bear it. "You were only sixteen, sweetheart," he said softly. "And that's not the kind of choice any sixteen-year-old should have to make, let alone punish herself over for so many years."

"But it was the wrong one." She couldn't stop the tears now; they were coming fast. Too many to blink away. Too many to pretend she wasn't crying. That her heart wasn't breaking. "I made the wrong choice. And I lost her, Connor. I lost her." The admission felt torn from her, a splinter of glass taking out what felt like the last piece of her soul. And she was breaking. Falling apart right in front of him.

Yet his arms came around her, taking her in a grip so strong, so certain it was as if he'd never let her go. Holding her together as she broke. Keeping her safe.

And she cried. All the pain she'd never let herself feel. All the anguish she'd been fighting for so many years. And the aching, aching regret that never went away.

After a long time, when all the tears she'd never let herself cry had finally ceased and she felt empty and cleaned out, light and fragile as a blown egg, she rested her head against his chest, listening to the deep, slow beat of his heart. "It's why I wanted to go to London," she said at last, her voice thick. "It's why I pushed myself in my career. That was my crusade. I had to make that choice mean something."

"I understand that, but you can't keep punishing yourself for a decision you made when you were sixteen, Victoria." His voice was a deep rumble in her ear. "If you want a crusade, if you want to make giving her up mean something, then it's not career success you should be pursuing."

She lifted her head at that and looked up at him. "Then what?"

He touched her hair, his palm sliding around to the back of her head, cradling her. "Passion. Happiness. Love. Even all of the above." He smiled, slow and brilliant. A smile she'd never seen before. "We're not our parents and their expectations. We're ourselves. We can make our own rules, set our own expectations. We can decide who we want to be." His smile deepened. "And who I want to be is your husband."

Damn lawyers and their excellent arguments. "Connor…"

"What about you? Who do you want to be, Victoria? What do *you* want?"

She'd thought she'd come to the end of her tears. She was wrong. Her eyes felt hot and prickly, her throat aching. He'd always been a brilliant man. She just hadn't ever imagined quite how brilliant. "I want to be worthy."

"It's not about worthiness. It's about acceptance." His fingers caught her chin, holding her firmly. "Do you love me?"

For a second she wished she could lie. But there was no lying about the feeling that curled around her bones, twining around her soul. That had grown too big now for denial. "Yes." The word came out as a croak.

"Then love me. And let me love you in return."

Eleanor was right. It was simple. He was here. And she wanted him. Just him, nothing more, nothing less.

"When we first got married, I thought you were the safe option," she said shakily. "You were intellectual and ambitious and that was very attractive to me. But then, two years ago, I saw you in court and you were… God, I'd never seen anything like it. All this passion seemed to come out of you, all this intensity. You seduced the jury into a guilty verdict and me right along with them. I wanted you so badly after that." She leaned into him, into the heat of his body. "It terrified me because I didn't want to feel like that, not for you, not for anyone. I thought if I ignored it I'd get over it and it would fade. But it never did." She swallowed. "I still feel it and I'm still afraid."

There was understanding in his eyes. "So am I. But we can do this, Victoria. I believe it and so should you."

Slowly, she let out a long breath and the last of her resistance along with it. "In that case..." Rising up on her toes, she pressed her mouth to his. "I love you," she whispered against his lips. "And I'll let you love me."

His arms tightened and he gave her his answer in a kiss that stole her breath and the last remains of her poor, battered heart.

And afterwards, when they were both breathless and aching, she said, "I can't go to London." She paused, knowing the truth of it like an incontrovertible fact. "I can't leave her again."

Connor didn't let her go. He only looked down at her with a tenderness that made her feel close to tears for the third time that day. "Then don't," he said softly.

So she didn't.

Turned out they both had a new crusade: happiness.

Epilogue

Victoria smoothed her dress for what was probably the fourth time in as many minutes. Her palms were sweaty and her stomach was in knots, and she wanted to go to the bathroom yet again.

Connor's warm hand settled over one of hers and instantly the nerves calmed. She turned to find his understanding blue gaze on hers. "It'll be okay," he said.

They were sitting in the car outside the restaurant Jessica had specified, the street already busy with the lunchtime crowds.

"What if she doesn't turn up?" Victoria couldn't help asking. "What if she changed her mind? What if—"

"It'll be okay," he repeated and she could hear the conviction in his voice. "She'll be there."

It had taken her a good couple of weeks after her decision to stay in New Zealand to finally contact Jessica. And over the past three months the two of them had exchanged emails and a couple of awkward, fraught phone calls. But it had been Jessica who'd suggested they meet, and even though Victoria had been ecstatic at the time, she was sick with nerves now.

She turned her hand beneath Connor's, laced her fingers with his, letting the warmth of his touch work its steadying magic.

Three months they'd been together. She'd moved back in a couple of months ago and now they were starting to explore and rebuild a different kind of relationship. A different kind of marriage from the one they'd had before. It was exciting, challenging. Terrifying.

A bit like her decision to finally meet her daughter, the last piece in her new crusade to accept the past and move on. To accept herself and the decision she'd made.

"Okay," she said. "If you say so."

"I do say so."

"But what if she doesn't like me?"

"She will like you."

"But—"

Her words were cut off as Connor leaned over from the driver's seat and kissed her. "Stop," he murmured. "You're perfect. You're amazing. You're my sexy, dirty girl and I love you." He kissed her again. "Now get out of the car and go meet your daughter."

Victoria let the sweetness of his kiss wash away the nervousness. And when she drew back, she was calmer. "Okay," she said firmly, decisively. "I'll text you when I'm ready to go."

She put a hand on the door handle and got out, shutting the door behind her.

The sidewalk was full of people, the bustling hive of the city all around her.

Then someone said, "Victoria?"

She turned and met the uncertain dark eyes of the young woman coming toward her. Olive skin, black hair. Beautiful. So heartbreakingly beautiful.

The uncertainty vanished from the young woman's features, a tentative smile taking their place. "Hi," she said. "I'm Jessica."

About the Author

Jackie has been writing fiction since she was eleven years old. Mild mannered fantasy/SF/pseudo-literary writer by day, obsessive romance writer by night, she used to balance her writing with the more serious job of librarianship until a chance meeting with another romance writer prompted her to throw off the shackles of her day job and devote herself to the true love of her heart—writing romance. She particularly likes to write dark, emotional stories with alpha heroes who've just got the world to their liking only to have it blown wide apart by their kick-ass heroines.

She lives in Auckland, New Zealand with her husband, the inimitable Dr Jax, two kids, two cats and a couple of curious rats. When she's not torturing alpha males and their stroppy heroines, she can be found drinking chocolate martinis, reading anything she can lay her hands on, posting random crap on Twitter, or being forced to go mountain biking with her husband.

You can find Jackie here:

www.jackieashenden.com

@JackieAshenden

www.facebook.com/jackie.ashenden

If you'd like to be kept up to date with information on Jackie's new and upcoming releases, you can sign up to her newsletter—details are at www.jackieashenden.com

Finding his way out of the darkness could be the biggest fight of his life.

Living in Shadow
© 2014 Jackie Ashenden

Living In…, Book 1

Law professor Eleanor May is fine with taking over a class for a colleague on sabbatical. She's not so fine with the hot student who's always seated front and center. Once upon a time *she* was that student… and the scars remain eight years after it ended.

Yet this guy seems different from the others. Despite the alarm bells in her head warning her about history repeating itself, she is drawn toward the forbidden once again—even though this time it could consume her.

Lucien North's past is darker than the ink on his skin, a reminder of a time when survival was a fight to the death. Seducing his beautiful professor wasn't supposed to be part of his plan to put it behind him, but there's something about Eleanor that's gotten hold of him and won't let go.

Together they light up the night, but will their powerful desire lead them to love—or drag them both to the brink of disaster?

Warning: This book contains a younger man so hot he might scorch your fingertips, and forbidden lust so tempting, there's no point in trying to resist. Check your inhibitions at the door—it's WTFery 101 and class is in session.

Enjoy the following excerpt for Living in Shadow:

English legal history. Fuck, Luc was starting to hate this class. It was his own special brand of hell: a lecture theatre full of people and him in the middle row with a slowly intensifying hard-on. And all because Professor Eleanor May was writing something on the whiteboard and her little pencil skirt was pulling tight around her extremely delectable ass.

Luc glanced down at the laptop open on his desk. Anything so he didn't have to look at her. The screen was completely blank. He hadn't taken any notes whatsoever and they were almost done with the class.

Jesus. This was the third time in as many weeks he'd sat there, hard and aching, thinking things he shouldn't be thinking instead of taking notes. At this rate he wouldn't be passing the paper if he didn't get his head back into study mode, and since he had only a couple of semesters left before getting his law degree, failing a paper would be very bad indeed.

She was talking again, her husky voice filling the room, and he didn't want to look because he knew what he would see: a petite, fine-boned woman with golden-blonde hair in an elegant chignon. All feminine sophistication in a beautifully tailored pencil skirt of pale blue and a crisp white shirt, a small silver necklace around her neck. It made her seem fragile, yet the impression she gave off was anything but. Her gray eyes were as sharp as a steel blade and she walked as if she were ten feet tall and bulletproof. Like she was keeping everyone at a distance.

But not when she spoke. When she gave a lecture, her delicate face would light up and the impression of ice and steel and distance would vanish. She would look at everyone in the room as if they were all having a conversation together and she was interested in what they had to say. Becoming warm and approachable. And if questions were asked, she'd smile and it would be like the sun had come into the room.

Christ, he wanted some of that sun.

He'd been at Auckland University for four years, only spotting Eleanor May a couple of years after he'd started since she mainly taught postgraduate students. Even back then, he'd registered her but had dismissed the attraction. She was a professor. Polished and sophisticated and way too much like hard work for him. He preferred his pleasure easy to come by and undemanding, with women who didn't want anything more from him than a couple of orgasms. Definitely not complicated, and seducing Professor May had complicated written all over it.

And then she'd taken over his English legal history class from Professor Holmes who'd gone off on sabbatical. And every Thursday he'd found himself sitting in the same place, right down in the front of the class, in the middle of the row, so he could look at her.

So he could figure out what the hell he found so fucking fascinating about her.

Because it wasn't only her beauty, though she had plenty of that. He could find beauty anywhere these days and though he'd once glutted himself on it, it hadn't ultimately satisfied him.

No, she had more than that. Perhaps it was the sharp intelligence he saw in her eyes whenever she spoke. Or maybe it was the distance she projected, as if she were holding the world at bay. The kind of distance that made him want to close it. Touch her.

Or perhaps it was merely the contrast to all the other women he'd had up till this point. Women his own age or a couple of years younger. Who had no distance, no walls. Children, in many ways. Children who didn't even know they were alive. Which was fine because that was the way children should be. Yet, at the same time, they offered no secrets. No challenges.

Strange to find that was suddenly an issue, when challenges and secrets and complications were the last thing he wanted.

Whatever it was that fascinated him about Eleanor May, it made every lecture pure fucking torture.

Luc sat back in his seat, folding his arms. Watching her. Irritated with himself and his stupid fucking cock with its insistence on wanting a woman he wasn't allowed to have anyway.

She was reaching the part where she looked at each person in turn as she reiterated her main points, a tactic that worked well in drawing people in to what she was saying. Except that, for some reason, she never looked at him.

God, he was sick of that too.

He shifted on his seat, spreading himself out a little, pinning his gaze on her. She looked at his neighbor, then, like it always did, her gaze skipped him and went on down the row. As if he didn't even exist.

Oh fuck no. Not today. Today she was going to damn well look.

Perhaps she's not looking at you for a reason?

Well, whatever the hell that reason was, it was not happening today.

Luc raised his hand to his mouth and coughed.

And she looked; cool, gray eyes seeking the source of the sound. Meeting his head on.

The electric shock of the impact hit him like a plunge into an icy lake on a blistering-hot day. Echoing through him, all the way down to the soles of his feet.

He stared at her and she stared back and he saw it—he fucking saw it—a flare of reaction in her eyes. So fast and fleeting that if he hadn't already been aware of her with every inch of his being, he may have missed it. But it was there nonetheless.

She looked away quickly, but by that time it was too late. He heard the falter in her voice. He saw the slight flush to her cheeks.

He knew.

She'd *seen* him. And not the student. She'd seen the man.

A surge of heat went through him, vicious and wild. Winding the ache inside him even tighter than it was already. Fuck, he so did not need this. He didn't get obsessed with women. They came to him if they wanted him, and, shit, he was happy to oblige. No harm, no foul. No one got hurt and that was how he liked it.

But being attracted to his professor? Christ. This was against the rules and he was a great believer in rules. Pity his body didn't seem to give a shit.

She was finishing up now, the people around him starting to put their stuff away in preparation for leaving. But he didn't want to go. He wanted those cool eyes on him again. Wanted to see that flash of reaction again. Because he was sure it had been a reaction. To him.

As the people around him began to get to their feet, he watched her stand by the podium, fiddling around with her laptop. Not looking at him.

Fuck. He needed to know. He needed to see if he was right. And he wasn't going to be able to concentrate on anything else until he did.

Living in Sin
© 2014 Jackie Ashenden

Living In…, Book 2

At twenty, Lily Andrews has already lived a lifetime. Her battle with leukemia put her three years behind her ballet career, and now that the grueling treatment is behind her, she's eager to put her dancing shoes back on—literally and figuratively.

One man has been her personal light at the end of her tunnel, the one man she's sure will help her rekindle her passion for life. Kahu Winter. And she'll let nothing stand in the way of having him—not even Kahu himself.

When Kahu catches Lily sneaking into his club, the desire in her eyes tells him it's more than a delayed act of youthful rebellion. Her lively spirit calls to him, but Kahu is too cynical, too jaded, too broken for a sweet young thing like her.

But Lily won't take no for answer so he'll make her a deal: She's got one month to seduce him and after that, he's moving on—figuratively and literally.

There's just one thing he forgot to keep out of her reach. His heart…

Warning: This book contains a hot older man in need of some anti-cynicism pills, a snarky younger woman who's going to get past his defenses and make him beg, more forbidden lust, and naked ballet dancing. Advanced WTFery for experienced users only.

Enjoy the following excerpt for Living in Shadow:

"She's here again."

"Oh fuck, really?" Kahu Winter leaned back in his office chair and stared at Mike, the bouncer who'd been working the door at the Auckland Club for the last five years.

Mike, a huge Tongan guy who used to do a lot of pro-wrestling, folded his arms. "Yeah. And she says she wants to see you."

Since that's what she'd been saying for the past couple of nights, Kahu wasn't surprised. Jesus Christ. What a pain in the ass.

He had more important things to do than fuck about dealing with Rob's daughter. The guy was Kahu's business partner and would not be happy at the thought of his twenty-year-old daughter hassling for entry into one of Auckland's most exclusive private-member's clubs.

What the hell was she doing here? What the hell did she want?

"That's the third time this week." Kahu threw the pen he'd been toying with back down on his desk. "And I'm getting pretty fucking sick of it."

Mike was unimpressed. "Perhaps if you go out and see what she wants, she'll go away," he pointed out.

Not what Kahu wanted to hear. Christ, the last two nights he'd paid for a taxi to take her home and if she kept this up, it was going to start getting expensive.

Of course, he could go out there and speak to her. But he liked being manipulated even less than he liked being told what to do. And he *hated* being told what to do. Especially when the person doing the telling was a spoiled little twenty-year-old on some mysterious mission she wouldn't talk to anyone about other than him.

Jesus, it made him feel tired. And pretty fucking old.

"Goddamn. I'm going to have to speak to her, aren't I?"

Mike lifted a shoulder. "Up to you, boss."

Yeah, he was going to have to.

Cursing, Kahu shoved his chair back and got up. The work he was doing, going over the club's accounts, could wait. And he probably needed a break anyway.

In the corridor outside his office, he could hear the sounds of conversation from the Ivy Room, the club's main bar and dining area. Friday night and the place was packed with members having a post-work drink or seven.

The sound of success. Anita would have been so proud.

Yeah, but not so proud of the fact you're planning on ditching it, huh?

No, probably not. She'd left him the club thirteen years ago, when she'd first realized she was getting sick. A gift he'd promptly thrown back in her face by fucking off overseas, refusing to accept the responsibility or the reality of her illness. It had taken him five years to come to terms with it. To come back to New Zealand, to take on the club, and most importantly, to care for her. The lover who'd rescued him from the streets and given him the stars.

On the other hand, Anita was six months dead and what she didn't know wouldn't hurt her.

As he approached the club's entrance—a vaulted hallway with stairs leading to the upper floors, a parquet floor, and a chandelier dominating the space like a massive, glittering sun—people greeted him. Since he granted all memberships to the club personally, he knew everyone. Some more than others, of course, but he prided himself on the fact that he knew everyone's names at least.

He ostentatiously kissed the hand of a politician's wife, slapped the back of a well-known actor, air-kissed with a socialite and shook hands with an awestruck nobody. But then that's what the Auckland Club was like. Nobodies and somebodies, all mixing together. It appealed to his sense of irony. And, fuck, it was a nice distraction if nothing else.

Kahu pushed open the big blue door that was the club's famous entrance and stood in the doorway, looking down the stairs to the sidewalk. There were no lines of people waiting to get into the club since it was members only, but tonight a lone figure sat on the bottom step, her back to him.

It was mid-winter and cold, his breath like a dragon's, a white cloud in the night.

Not as cold as London, though.

A random memory drifted through his head, of the European "cultural" trip with Anita. Of being in London in February during a snowstorm, and she'd tried to insist on going to some kind of classical music concert at Covent Garden. He'd seduced her in their fancy Claridges hotel room instead and they'd spent the rest of the evening in bed, away from the storm and the cold...

Kahu let out another cloudy breath, trying to shake the memories away.

He'd grieved when Anita had died. But the woman in that chair in the rest home wasn't the Anita he'd known and loved. That woman had died a long time ago.

The person sitting down on the bottom step suddenly turned and his drifting thoughts scattered. A pale, pointed face and eyes an indeterminate color between green and gray looked back at him. A familiar face.

Lily.

He knew her, of course. Had known her since she was about five years old, her father Rob being a close friend of Anita's, and who'd managed the club while Kahu had been sulking overseas. Who'd become a valued business partner since.

A quiet, watchful girl who stayed out of the way and did what she was told, if he remembered right. He hadn't seen her for five years, though, and clearly things had changed. Namely that she didn't do as she was told anymore.

Lily stood and turned around. She was wearing a black duffel coat, the hood pulled up against the cold, and dark skinny jeans, a pair of Chuck Taylors covered with Union Jacks on her feet. And a very determined look on her face.

"Lily Andrews, as I live and breathe," Kahu said lazily, standing in the doorway of his club and crossing his arms. "Does your father know you've been sitting on the steps of my club for the past three nights straight?"

Her hands pushed into the pockets of her coat, brows the color of bright flames descending into a frown. "If you'd spoken to me earlier it wouldn't have been three nights."

"I have a phone. Though perhaps young people these days don't use such outdated technology."

"What I want to ask you is better done in person."

"That sounds portentous. Come on then, don't keep me in suspense. What do you want?"

She didn't speak immediately, her mouth tightening, her eyes narrowing. As if she was steeling herself for something.

Jesus, whatever it was it had better be good. He had shit to do.

After a brief, silent moment, Lily walked up the steps, coming to stand in front of him. The light coming from the club's doorway shone directly on her face. She wore no makeup, her skin white, almost translucent and gleaming with freckles like little specks of gold. She looked sixteen if she was a day.

"Can I come in? I don't want to ask you out here."

"What, into the club? Sorry, love, but it's members only."

She shifted restlessly on her feet. "So can I be a member then?"

"Are you kidding? You think I just hand out membership to any fool that comes to my door?"

Her forehead creased into a scowl. "I'm not a fool."

"If you're not a fool, then you'll understand that there's a reason it's taken me three days to speak to you."

"I just want to ask you a question. Nothing else."

"Then send me an e-mail or a text like any normal teenager. Now, if you don't mind, I have a few things I—"

"I'm not a teenager, for Christ's sake. And what I want to talk to you about is…personal."

Kahu leaned against the doorframe, eyeing her. "If it's personal then why aren't you talking to your dad or a friend or whatever? You hardly know me."

Rob had been Anita's lawyer as well as her friend. Kahu had met him in the context of dinners, where Anita had brought Kahu along and he'd sat there silently at the table while she and Rob talked, unable to join in because he didn't know what the fuck they were talking about—the dumb, uneducated Maori kid from the streets.

Sometimes at those dinners Lily had been there, a small seven-year-old with big eyes, whom he'd ignored mainly because she was a child and he had nothing to say to a privileged white kid from Remuera, born with a silver spoon in her mouth.

Then, after he'd come back from overseas and had reconnected with Rob over the management of the Auckland Club, he'd sometimes see her as he talked business with her father. A slender teen with a sulky mouth, who appeared to lurk permanently in the hallway whenever he arrived or left, big gray-green eyes following him when she thought he wouldn't notice.

She'd grown up a bit since then, the rounded features of adolescence morphing into the more defined lines of adulthood. But that mouth of hers was still sulky and she was still small and slender. And her eyes were still wide and big as they met his.

"Yeah, I realize that. But…" She shifted again, nervous. "What I want to ask concerns you in particular."

He raised an eyebrow. "Me, huh? Well, spit it out then."

A crowd of people came up the steps behind her, laughing and talking. Kahu moved out of the way as they approached the door, greeting them all by name and holding out his arm to usher them inside.

Once they'd all gone in, he turned back to Lily, who remained standing there with her hands in the pockets of her coat, glaring at him almost accusingly.

He could not, for the life of him, work out what her problem was, but one thing was for sure: he was getting bloody sick of standing there while she continued to dance around the subject.

"Okay," he said, glancing at his watch. "You've got ten seconds. If you haven't told me what you're doing here by then, I'm going to go inside and ring your father, and ask him to come and get you."

"All right, Jesus," Lily muttered. "You don't have to be such a dick about it."

Kahu refrained from rolling his eyes. "Ten, nine, eight, seven…"

She turned her head, looking back down the steps, clearly checking to make sure there was no one around.

"…six, five, four, three—"

"I was kind of wondering if you could perhaps seduce me."

SAMHAIN
PUBLISHING

It's all about the story...

Romance

HORROR

Retro
ROMANCE

www.samhainpublishing.com